The Hunter

The Hunter

JOHN R. ERICKSON

DOUBLEDAY & COMPANY, INC.
GARDEN CITY, NEW YORK
1984

All of the characters in this book
are fictitious, and any resemblance
to actual persons, living or dead,
except for actual historical personages,
is purely coincidental.

Library of Congress Cataloging in Publication Data

Erickson, John R., 1943–
The hunter.

I. Title.
PS3555.R428H8 1984 813'.54

ISBN: 0-385-18897-8
Library of Congress Catalog Card Number 83–45007

Printed in the United States of America
First Edition

The Hunter

Part One

The Wild Man

1

It all seemed so inevitable. He would marry Martha Wynn. They would move into the second floor of the Valkenburg mansion. He would take over the management of the Valkenburg properties. They would be set for life. What more could a young man want in Weatherford, Texas, in 1873?

Gil Moreland gazed out the window and watched the two big freight wagons move down the street. Each wagon was hitched to six yoke of oxen. They were loaded down with goods and heading west, toward Palo Pinto, Fort Griffin, and perhaps even beyond, to the edge of the frontier. They carried powder and shot, flour and bacon and salt pork for the buffalo hunters; whiskey and beer for the soldiers at the fort; cloth and lace and thread for the wives of the officers; paint and perfume for the women of the dance halls and whiskey mills.

The wagons moved on down the street. Gil's eyes returned to the room and to the three women seated in the parlor: Mrs. Valkenburg, the small, spry, silver-haired lady who had taken him into her home thirteen years ago when the Comanches had left him an orphan; Mrs. Hubert Wynn, Jr., soon to be his mother-in-law; and Martha, her daughter. They had spent the last two hours planning the wedding and the feast that would follow. Gil had not said a word, and he wondered why Mrs. Valkenburg had insisted that he be present.

Martha cast him a shy glance, smiled, and looked away. She was rather tall and willowy, had long hair the color of ripe wheat, and the clearest blue eyes one could imagine. She played the piano, read poetry and the Bible. She, like her mother, was a solid Methodist. She could cook and sew and can. Everyone in Weatherford agreed that she would make Gil an excellent wife.

He yawned behind his hand and noticed a smudge of dirt on the gold band he wore on his little finger. He scraped it off with his thumbnail and polished the ring on his shirt. It had been his mother's wedding band, and she had given it to him on her deathbed. She had intended for him to give it to the girl he chose to marry, but he had decided not to give it to Martha. He would buy one for her and keep his mother's ring for himself.

The ladies were making out the guest list now. He noticed that Mrs. Wynn's double chin trembled when she talked. He hoped that double chins were not hereditary and that Martha would not develop one.

He heard a knock at the front door. Mrs. Valkenburg stopped talking and started to rise from her chair. Gil jumped to his feet. "I'll get it."

"Oh, would you mind?" she said, and plunged back into the discussion. Martha gave him a smile, as though she understood that he was getting restless.

He crossed the room with long strides and closed the parlor door behind him. Out in the hall he stretched his arms and breathed a sigh of relief. He had been sitting for an hour and a half, and his body ached for some activity.

Pearl, the Negro maid, had already answered the door. She had pulled it half-closed and stood with her hands on her hips in the opening. The caller was a man. Gil couldn't see him, since Pearl's broad, squat body stood in the way, but he could hear his voice. Pearl was giving him a hard time, as she often did to strangers, and it didn't take her long to send him on his way. She closed the door and dusted her hands together, a gesture she used to indicate that she had cleaned up another mess.

"Who was it, Pearl?"

"I don't know, didn't ask his name, didn't want to. He looked like trash to me, and don't nobody in Missa Falconbird's house have no use for trash."

"What do you mean, 'trash'? Was he a beggar or a peddler?"

She scowled. "No, but I can tell trash when I see it. He look like one of them kind that just come in from the frontier, wid a greasy leather shirt and a smell like a billy goat."

"What did he want?"

"I didn't ast, but I could tell right off that we didn't have no use for his kind in this house." She started back to the kitchen. "I never did trust no man wit dirty fingernails."

Gil opened the door and went out on the porch. The stranger was just going out the yard gate. Gil called to him, and he came back to the house. He wore a full red beard, a wide-brimmed hat, a pair of heavy leather boots, and a leather hunting shirt. As Pearl had said, his dress and aroma marked him as a man of the frontier.

Gil knew that he had seen this man before. He remembered the small greenish eyes and the short, powerful arms, the stubby hands and the short chin. Yet he couldn't pull a name from his memory.

"I'm sorry Pearl sent you away," said Gil. "What is it that you wanted?"

The stranger looked him up and down with narrowed eyes. "I'm looking for Peter Valkenburg. Do the Valkenburgs still live in this house? It's been a while since I was here."

"This is the Valkenburg home, but I'm sorry to say that Mr. Valkenburg passed away last September."

"I'm sorry to hear that."

"But Mrs. Valkenburg is here, if you'd like to see her."

The man smiled. "No, thanks just the same. I was a friend of Peter's, but the missus never quite approved of me. And who might you be, young man?"

"My name is Gil Moreland."

His eyes widened. "No, you don't say! The lad whose family was killed by the Indians? Why, you're a grown man now, and a right handsome devil, I would add."

"And who are you, sir? I should know you, but I can't recall your name."

"Ben Woolsey, lad. Have you already forgotten the man who led the soldiers into the Pease River country and found the Comanche devils? I'm the man who had the pleasure of putting a lead ball into the heart of your mother's killer, and then wearing his scalp on my belt."

"Ben!" Gil cried. "Of course it's you!" He took Woolsey's rough hand and gave it a shake. "It's been such a long time, and you've changed."

"And you've changed yourself, lad, though in a much kinder way than I. Why, you're a very devil of a man, as big as a yearling ox. Your ma would sure be proud to see you now."

"Ben, please come in. You look hot and tired."

"I am, fresh from the frontier and dying of thirst. Go with me to a nice watering spot and we'll talk about the old times. I wouldn't feel comfortable in the house."

"All right, Ben, let's . . ."

Mrs. Valkenburg appeared at the door. Her dark blue eyes went straight to Ben Woolsey. "Who is it, Gil?"

"This is Ben Woolsey, don't you remember him? The scout and frontiersman who brought me to this house the day I came to live with you."

Mrs. Valkenburg nodded her head and continued to stare at Ben. "Yes, of course. Hello, Mr. Woolsey. I judge that you've had a hard life since we saw you last."

"Yes ma'am, I suppose I have."

There was an awkward silence. "Mother, Ben just came to town and I was going to help him find a room for the night."

"I would imagine that he can find his own room. Perhaps tomorrow would be a better day to see him. We have plans to make. Gil is getting married, Mr. Woolsey." She turned her gaze on Gil. "When Mr. Woolsey leaves, I'm sure you'll want to offer us your advice on the guest list. Good afternoon, Mr. Woolsey. It was kind of you to stop by and say hello."

She gave him a polite smile, glanced at Gil, and went back into the house.

Ben whistled under his breath. "Didn't know it could get so cold in the middle of summer."

"I'm sorry, Ben. She's that way with everyone, not just you." Ben grunted, as though he knew better. "I'll have to stay here for a while. Go to the Keechi Saloon and order what you want. It's on me tonight. I'll join you as soon as I can get away."

Ben nodded and left, and Gil returned to the parlor. Through the window he saw Ben climb on a thin bay horse and ride down the street toward the town square. When he looked away from the window, he met Mrs. Valkenburg's blue eyes. She didn't ask him about the guest list or about anything else, but for the next hour she continued to watch him, as though she expected that he might try to slip out of the room.

She was very perceptive when she wanted to be. She could read a face like a book. She had seen something in his face out on the porch, and he could tell that it disturbed her.

2

At six o'clock Martha and her mother finally said good-bye and left the house. They both wore hats and shawls, even though the day was quite warm, and their dresses were so long, only the toes of their shoes showed when they walked.

Mrs. Valkenburg closed the door and turned to Gil. "Martha Wynn is an exceptionally fine young lady. She has poise and good sense."

"Yes, she does."

"And she seems to fit into any situation."

"Yes, she does indeed." Gil could feel his pocket watch ticking away the seconds. If she would just walk into the other room, he would slip out the door and join Ben at the Keechi.

"Martha and Mrs. Wynn are working hard to make this a beautiful wedding. It will be the biggest wedding in Weatherford's history. Dr. Wynn has many friends."

He nodded. She was still blocking the door. "Well, I think I'll go upstairs and change. Excuse me."

He walked through the sitting room and started up the stairs. Mrs. Valkenburg followed him to the foot of the stairs. He could feel her eyes on him.

"What time should I tell Pearl to have supper?"

He stopped at the first landing and looked down at her.

She stood with her hands clasped at her waist, her back straight, her head held at that distinctive Valkenburg angle. "I'm not very hungry. You and Pearl go ahead and eat without me."

She turned on her heel and walked away without a word. She knew where he was going.

He took the remaining steps two at a time, went to his room, and closed the door. He stripped off his coat, vest, and white shirt and tossed them in a pile on the floor, then added his pants to the heap. Pearl would pick them up tomorrow. He pulled on a pair of cotton breeches and a shirt with two rows of buttons along the front. Then he slipped on his high-topped leather boots, which looked very much like the ones Ben had worn. He ran a brush through his long blond hair and curled up the ends of his mustache.

Mrs. Valkenburg had never approved of the mustache, neither the fiery red color nor the length nor the way he twisted up the ends so that they resembled the horns of a bull. But he liked it and had kept it. Over the years, he had rarely defied her, but on the matter of the mustache he had stood his ground. The mustache belonged to him and he would never cut it off.

He went to the door and opened it a crack and listened. He could hear Mrs. Valkenburg talking to Pearl downstairs. He closed the door and went to the open window on the south. He stepped out on the ledge and stretched out his long frame until he seized a sturdy limb on the mimosa tree. He pushed himself off the ledge and swung until he was able to wrap a leg around the limb and pull himself down the trunk. From there he dropped to the ground, ducked behind a juniper hedge and trotted around to the back of the house. He was out of sight now, and he raised up and trotted toward the town square.

It was dark inside the Keechi Saloon, and it was beginning to fill up with the evening trade, mostly freighters and transients who were on their way to or from the settlements to the west. Ben Woolsey sat at a table in the far corner, facing the door. He was sawing on a piece of beefsteak and shoveling it into his mouth, first with his knife and then with his fork. When he saw Gil, he waved the knife in the air.

"Sit down, lad," he kicked out a chair. "I was too hungry to wait supper for you, but would you have a drink with me?" Gil said he would, and Ben waved his knife at the bartender. "Whiskey, sir, a bottle and two glasses." When the bartender brought them, Ben uncorked the bottle with his teeth and spit it on the floor. "You go slow and keep yourself respectable, lad. Don't try to stay up with old Ben, because old Ben is liable to get his feet tangled tonight." He threw a splash of liquor into Gil's glass and poured his own half full. He tossed it down in one gulp, growled with pleasure as his eyes filled with tears, and wiped his mouth with the sleeve of his shirt. "My God, that's"—he coughed—"good!"

Gil took a sip. "Ben, it's good to see you again. Where are you coming from, where are you going? Tell me about the frontier. I want to hear everything."

Ben looked at him and smiled. "You always did like my yarns. I remember you as a pup. I never could tell you enough stories about the West. Well, I'll tell you a few tonight, but first let me finish my grain and hay."

He stuffed half the remaining steak into his mouth. His cheeks bulged and grease ran out the corners of his mouth and into his beard. Had Mrs. Valkenburg witnessed such barbaric enthusiasm over food, she would have had to go to bed for two days to recover. Ben chewed and pulled pieces of bone and tendon out of his mouth. At last he conquered the steak and swallowed a lump so large that it made his eyes bulge as it went down. He sighed and burped, wiped his hands on his pant legs, pushed the plate away, and rested his elbows on the table.

"So you want a good story? Well, I've got one, lad, that beats any I ever told or heard, and I'll swear by the Christ that every word of it is the truth."

Ben leaned back in his chair and propped his boots up on the edge of the table. The saloon was crowded with men who were laughing and talking, but Gil was hardly aware of them. His gaze was fixed on Ben Woolsey.

"Back in the fall of seventy-two," he began, "I found myself in country west of here. I was fresh from the buffalo range on the Republican River in Kansas and had made a dangerous trip through the Panhandle. It was the wildest, loneliest country I ever saw, lad. When I left the settlements on the Arkansas River in Kansas, I didn't see another white face until I reached Clear Fork of the Brazos.

"Have you ever heard of Fort Phantom Hill?" Gil shook his head. "It was a military garrison, built during the Mexican War and then abandoned a few years later. The old stone buildings are still standing near Clear Fork. I had never heard of the place myself, but I stumbled onto it as I was making my way toward the settlements. I smelled the smoke of cooking fires and rode up to it. I didn't know what to expect, so I had my old six-shooting Remington near at hand.

"What I found was a small community of people who had moved into the old fort. It was a small town, you might say, out there in the middle of nowhere. These people were hunters and trappers, for the most part, who had reasons for leaving civilization. Some had deserted from the Civil War. Some had left their homes to escape the law. Some were there to find adventure. They were a rough-and-tumble lot, both men and women, and I felt right at home.

"This was November. There was already a chill in the air and winter was coming on, and since I had no place special to go and nothing in mind to do, I decided to stay until spring and run a trapline.

"I made a trip to Fort Griffin and bought my supplies at the suttler's store. By the first of December, the weather had turned cool enough to set the hair on a pelt, and I was ready to lay out my trapline. One afternoon, when I was putting my gear together, a Mexican fellow walked up to me and asked if anybody had told me about the wild man. I said no. He said there was a wild man living in the Clear Fork country. 'A wild man?' says I. 'And what in the name of the devil is a *wild man?*' He shrugged his shoulders and walked away.

"I didn't think much about it. Mexicans tend to be superstitious, if you ask me, and a man doesn't want to believe everything they say. But then someone else asked me the same question: had I heard about the wild man? By this time my curiosity was up and I said, 'No, friend, I don't know about the wild man, but maybe you ought to tell me.'

"He claimed that there was a creature out there on the prairie who walked on two legs and had the features of a man, but he lived with the animals. The animals weren't afraid of him. He'd been seen by a number of people, and the trappers knew all about him because he robbed their traps and let the animals go. The trappers hated him and had sworn to kill him on sight. But somehow they never got the job done."

Ben paused and took a drink of whiskey. "I've been around, I've seen a good chunk of this old world, and I'm not the kind who scares easy. I didn't believe the yarn and figured somebody was trying to scare off the competition. Around the fifteenth of December, I loaded up my gear on two packhorses and rode up Clear Fork to lay out my trapline. It took me the better part of a week. I made some trail sets and some bait sets and some scent sets. I was after wolf and bobcat, since those pelts brought the most money, but I wasn't opposed to taking a few coyotes and coons and badgers. I'd just as soon leave the badgers to someone else—they stink and the hide's awful greasy—but you get a few of them, whether you want them or not.

"I ran my line twice a week. It took me a full day to check the traps and make new sets. I'd take the catch back to Phantom Hill, skin and stretch hides for a couple of days, and then ride the line again. This was a pretty fresh country, hadn't been trapped much, and I had good luck. By Christmas I had a good stack of hides piled up. But then my luck ran out. I wasn't catching anything, and it was kind of strange. I'd find all the traps sprung, and sometimes there would be fresh animal sign around the spot, as though I'd caught something and he'd gotten away. It wasn't hardly natural."

Ben looked at Gil and arched his brows. "Then I started finding these footprints. They were made by a man, and they went from one trap to another, all the way down the line. I thought maybe someone at Phantom Hill was robbing my traps, so I started keeping a sharp eye out. Then one day as I was riding along, I happened to look back over my shoulder"—he took another drink—"and got my first look at the wild man."

Gil had been listening to every word of the story, leaning across the table so that he could hear over the noise. "You saw him?"

Ben nodded. "I saw him, with these two eyes, and he was just as real as you are."

"What did he look like?"

"He was big, your size or maybe even bigger. Powerful shoulders, barrel chest, muscular arms and legs, no fat. His hair was coal black and so long that it reached halfway down his back. What chilled me were his eyes." Ben leaned forward and lowered his voice. "They weren't human, lad. They was the eyes of a wolf, as yellow as the blazing sun."

"What did you do when you saw him?"

"What did I do? Well, he stared at me and I stared at him. Neither of us moved for maybe a minute or two. He made some kind of grunting noise. I ran a spur halfway through my horse and got the hell out of there just as fast as I could. I didn't slow down until I got back to Phantom Hill. I told some men what I'd seen, and they said, yep, that was the wild man, all right. Four of us rode out the next day —heavily armed, as you might imagine—and picked up the trail. We followed it for a mile and then it just disappeared."

"Did you trap any more?"

Ben laughed. "Well, I did more or less. You can't run a trapline when you're looking back over your shoulder all the time, or when somebody's robbing your traps. I stayed with it until the middle of January, didn't have much luck. About that time, one of my trapping friends, a guy named Lonnie from Mississippi, came in one day all beat up and scratched. The wild man had jumped him, gave him a pretty severe thrashing. I didn't need any of that, so I just sort of retired for the season. So did everybody else."

Gil studied Ben's weathered face, searching for some sign that the story might have been manufactured. But the face was as honest as a rock. "That's quite a story, Ben. I've never heard anything like it."

He grinned, revealing a row of brown-stained teeth and narrowing his eyes to slits. "Back when you was a boy, I told you a few windies and stretched the truth just a wee bit. But this story about the wild man didn't need no help. It's all true."

Gil started to say something when he noticed that a

change had come over Ben's face. The smile was gone, and he was looking toward the front door.

"What's wrong?"

"An old acquaintance of mine just walked in. Sit tight and don't look around. I can't tell whether he's looking for me or not." He reached into his vest and brought something out of his waistband. Gil caught a glimpse of blue steel. It was a pistol. Ben laid it across his lap and held it there, out of sight. "If I give the word, you hit the floor and lay flat until the smoke clears."

Gil felt pin pricks on the back of his neck. He wanted to look around and see the "acquaintance," but Ben had told him not to. He sat still and waited, and watched the lines of tension on Ben's face.

3

Half an hour passed. Ben didn't take his eyes off the man, not even for a second.

"His name's Trumbull. I knew him up in Kansas. He calls himself a buffalo hunter and he runs with that rough crowd, but he ain't a hunter. He's a thief and a killer and he lives off other people. You don't ever want to turn your back on his kind."

"Why is he looking for you?"

"I don't know that he is. Could be just coincidence that I'm here and so is he. Met him in a buffalo camp on the Republican River. One afternoon when I was supposed to be out on a hunt, I went back to camp and caught him going through my belongings. I'm satisfied that he was looking for money. I called him a thief and he went for his artillery. I got there first and brought him down with a leg shot. While he was down, I went over and marked him."

"Marked him?"

"Cut off the top of his ear. You'll see it if he comes over here, which I reckon he will, sooner or later. He's over there arm rassling with a couple of bullwhackers, but he seen me as soon as he walked in the door."

"Are you going to shoot it out with all these people around?"

"That sort of depends on Trumbull, lad. I'm just playing it safe. We'll know here in a minute. He's coming this way."

Trumbull was smiling when he walked up to the table. He cast a careless glance at Gil and then turned to Ben. He was a powerfully built man, about six feet tall and so thick in the shoulders that he had hardly any neck at all. His upper body tapered down to a thin waist and a pair of legs that seemed too short and thin for the rest of his frame. His broad face was covered with whiskers, and he had a pair of small black eyes.

And the top half of his right ear was missing.

"This must be my lucky night," he said to Ben. "I come to Texas and right off I find one of my old friends from the buffalo range. Ain't that luck?"

"If you say so."

"You didn't follow me all the way to Texas, did you Woolsey?"

"I got here first. Maybe you followed me."

"Not likely. If I'd been following you, you never would have got here."

"Maybe. Or you wouldn't have."

Trumbull laughed. "There's always that chance. Sooner or later one of us is likely to turn up missing. That's a poor way to live, when a man gets himself all grudged up like that. It goes against my nature to bear a grudge, but you know, Ben, every time I look in a mirror, I think about you."

"That's good, Trumbull, I'm glad to hear it. Think of me and remember that Ben Woolsey hates a thief."

Trumbull turned to Gil and looked him over. There was a pushy, probing quality in his stare that made Gil uncomfortable. "Is this your kid?" he asked Ben.

"He's a friend."

"Well, ain't you even going to interdoose me? Name's C. D. Trumbull." He offered his hand.

"Don't take it, Gil," said Ben.

Trumbull turned back to Ben. "What are you worried about? I can see that you got the goods in your lap there, and I ain't even carrying sidearms." He lifted his vest and turned around so that Ben could see that he wasn't armed.

"What about the knife in your boot top?"

Trumbull grinned. "My toothpick? It wouldn't hurt nobody." He reached into his boot and brought out a six-inch butcher knife and laid it on the table. "There, that better? Let's arm rassle, Woolsey, just for old times."

"No thanks."

"S'matter, you scared?"

"Yeah."

"You always was a little chickenhearted when it came to a fair fight. Come on. I'll even go lefties with you. You're lefthanded, you ought to win on lefties."

"No thanks."

Trumbull's gaze drifted over to Gil. "How about you, Pretty Boy? You're a big stout lad. Let's see how you match up with an old buck, the arm rassling king of the buffalo camps."

Gil was about to refuse when he noticed a crooked smile on Ben's mouth. "Go ahead, lad, see what you can do."

Both men were staring at him. Other men in the saloon had drifted over to the table and were waiting to see what he would say. "Well, all right." It had been years since he had arm wrestled and he had no idea how well he would do against Trumbull. But he didn't intend to humiliate himself in front of all these men.

Trumbull dragged up a chair and sat down across the table from him. He removed the wide-brimmed hat from his head, exposing a pate that was as slick and hairless as an egg. He plunked his arm down on the table and grinned. "I just love fresh meat. Let's go."

Gil rolled up the right sleeve of his shirt and fitted his hand into Trumbull's, and felt the thick fingers close like a vise. Gil gripped the corner of the table with his left hand. Trumbull was already putting pressure on his arm, trying to get an advantage.

"I think we're supposed to start with the arms straight up and down, Mr. Trumbull."

Trumbull laughed. "It don't matter to me, 'cause I'm gonna take yours plumb out of the socket in just a minute. You ready?"

Gil took a deep breath and set his jaws. "Ready."

"Go!"

Trumbull had tremendous strength in his hand and arm, and he went for a quick victory. He pushed Gil's arm toward the table. But Gil had a slight advantage in that his arm was longer than Trumbull's. If he could just survive that first burst of strength, he might be able to wear the older man down and win on endurance.

Trumbull's teeth were set together and his lips were spread apart. The veins in his face and neck bulged under the strain and his breath whistled in his nostrils. Gil was losing ground. Trumbull sensed that the victory was his and strained harder. The crowd had grown larger and the men were beginning to cheer. Most of the cheering was for Gil, the hometown boy. He tried to resist the crushing strength in Trumbull's hand, but his arm moved closer and closer to the table.

Then, only three inches from the table, their arms stopped. Trumbull grunted. Both men's arms quivered under the strain. Beads of sweat glistened on Trumbull's bald head. A glassy look appeared in his eyes, and Gil began to gain back some of the ground he had lost. The crowd cheered. Their arms were straight up and down now, and Trumbull was breathing hard. He had lost some of his grip.

"You want to call it a draw?" he said between his clenched teeth.

"No."

Trumbull curled his lip and threw all his strength into one last effort. Gil held his ground. Trumbull's hand went limp and Gil smashed it over against the table. A cheer went up. The big man shot Gil a murderous glare, murmured something with his lips, snatched up his knife and hat, and stalked out of the saloon. The hoots and jeers of the crowd followed him out.

Some of the spectators came up and slapped Gil on the back. One man brought him a beer and set it down in front of him. He was happy and surprised that he had won. His arm and hand were so weak from the struggle that he couldn't lift the glass of beer.

Ben Woolsey hadn't said anything about the victory, but he wore a smile and there was an admiring gleam in his eyes. When the crowd drifted away, he stuffed his pistol back into his waistband, took Gil's right hand, and looked it over as though he were examining a piece of machinery or a weapon he had never seen before.

"You're a whole lot stouter than a man would think, if he judged you by the clothes you wear. You just beat one of the best." He moved his hand up Gil's arm, feeling the muscles. "Yeah, you're well muscled. They're good firm muscles, not real bulky but hard. I thought he had you beat, and to tell you the truth, I would have bet against you. But you stayed in there and didn't let him outstout you at the first. It was a nice piece of work."

"Thanks."

"But I'll tell you something. You'd better keep an eye out for Trumbull from now on. He won't forget, and one of these nights he's just liable to step out of the shadows and try to bend a piece of iron around your head."

"Why? It was his idea, and I beat him fair and square."

"That's the way me and you would look at it, lad, but Trumbull ain't like me and you. Just be aware and don't ever let him come up on your blind side. When you get as old as I am, you'll realize that there's a very small difference between being alive and being dead. It all comes down to inches and seconds."

Gil opened and closed his right hand until he felt his grip return. He hoisted his glass of beer and took a long drink. "Where are you heading, Ben?"

"Oh, I don't know. I'm kind of torn two ways right now. One day I'll wake up and feel the aches in my joints and I'll think, 'Ben, you're marching up on fifty years of age and here you are, sleeping on the hard ground and living the wild life. Why don't you just give it up, find a nice little farm some place, and finish out your life on a feather bed?'

"But then, damn it all, I get up and work out the stiffness and start thinking that there's only one place for me, and that's out on the frontier. That's what I was telling myself today when I knocked on your door. Me and Mr. Valkenburg went partners on a few deals, and I thought I'd see if he wanted to stake me for a season of trapping. But he's dead."

There was a long pause. "I'll stake you."

Ben's eyes came up. "You?"

Gil nodded. "I have the money. I'll finance you at no interest, if you'll agree to two small conditions."

"Ordinarily, I don't like conditions."

"These aren't bad. The first is that I'm going with you and you're going to teach me about hunting and trapping and life on the frontier."

Ben grunted and took a drink. "What's the other one?"

"We'll locate at Phantom Hill."

Ben stared at him for a long time, his mouth half open. "What you got on your mind, lad?"

"I want to catch the wild man."

"Heh." He took a drink and looked away. "I'm afraid I'll have to pass."

"If we caught the wild man, you'd have good trapping on Clear Fork."

Ben only smiled, and the subject was dropped. Ben went on drinking and they talked about old times. Around eleven o'clock Ben rolled his glass around in his hand and stared at it with glazed eyes. "Why would you want to catch the wild man?"

"Just to see if I could do it."

"What about this big wedding? I thought you was getting married here in a few weeks."

"I've just realized that I'm not ready. I've always wanted to go to the frontier, and this is the time to do it."

"Could be."

"What do you say, Ben? I'll pay all the expenses and you can keep all the profit for your retirement."

"I need some fresh air." He grabbed the whiskey bottle by the neck and headed for the door. Outside, Gil fell in step beside him. Ben turned up the bottle and let it gurgle into his mouth. He was beginning to stagger. He finished the bottle and tossed it out into the street and started singing "Comin' Through the Rye."

"Ben, I think it would be exciting."

"What?"

"Catching the wild man."

"Oh, that. Could be." They walked on down the dark street. At the end of the block, Ben stopped and steadied himself on a white picket fence. "You better run along, lad. I've got some prowling to do, and I can't use no help."

"All right, Ben. It was good seeing you again."

"Yeah, same here. Take care of yourself."

Gil walked on down the street, until he heard Ben call "Hey!" He turned around and went back. "You serious about going west?"

"Yes."

"And you'd banker the deal and I'd get the furs?"

"That's right."

He shook his head. "Naw, better not. Run along home."

Gil walked away again, and once again Ben called out. He stopped, but this time he let Ben come to him. He came lurching down the dirt path, frowning and holding one finger in the air. "Now, let's go over that one more time. Are you saying that you'd pay all the expenses and I'd keep all the profits?" Gil nodded. "That don't make sense. I don't see how I could lose."

"You can't lose. It's a good deal for you. Will you take it?"

"Naw, I don't think . . . naw, I just . . . tell you what let's do. Meet me at the livery barn in two days." He counted off the days on his fingers. "Friday morning. I'll be done prowling by then. We'll talk. But don't get your hopes up, because the chances are that I'll . . . I'll get *all* the profits, you say?"

Gil smiled. "See you in two days, Ben." He turned and walked away.

"Hey! You done all right with old Trumbull. I was proud."

He lurched away. Gil wondered if he would ever see him again.

4

It was past midnight when Gil slipped into the house and closed the door behind him. He removed his boots so that his feet wouldn't make any noise on the wood floor. He didn't see Mrs. Valkenburg until he was right beside her.

She was sitting in her favorite chair in the living room and had probably been waiting there in the darkness for hours.

"Where have you been?"

Would he lie or tell her the truth? "I've been talking with Ben Woolsey."

"I thought you had."

"I hope to be leaving with him in a few days. I'll be gone a long time."

"I thought you would."

"I know you're disappointed in me, and I'm sorry."

There was a long silence. "I kept you as long as I could, Gil, but I had begun to suspect that your heart was somewhere else. Are you sure that leaving is the right thing?"

"Yes, I'm sure."

"Then go, and God bless you. I'll pray for your safe return."

He hardly knew what to say. He knelt down and laid his head across her lap. "Thank you, Mother."

She stroked his head and ran her fingers through his long hair. "You're not my true flesh and blood, Gil, but I couldn't have loved you more if you had been. I'll always love you, my son, and when you've seen what you must see, come back home and I'll be sitting in this chair, watching for you through the window."

"I'll come back."

She took his head in her arms and held it to her breast. He felt a drop of moisture on the back of his neck. It was a tear, but she didn't cry. "You must talk to Martha tomorrow."

"I know. I'm dreading it."

"It won't be so bad, as long as you tell her the truth. She'll understand that it's better for her. But don't expect her to wait for you. She's ready to marry and there are many young men who would be proud to have her. Now go to bed and sleep. You have my blessing."

Gil kissed her on the cheek and said good night. She remained in her chair in the dark room.

The next day he waited until after lunch to go over to the Wynn house. It was a large white house that stood at the end of a wooded lane, and beyond it lay the rolling prairie country. You could see the West from their front porch.

He saw her in the yard. He paused and watched her. She wore a long blue dress and a blue sunbonnet to match. She was bending over a flower bed beside the front step. He admired the graceful curve of her back and her slender arm. He knew it was wrong to have carnal thoughts about a lady, but he had often wondered what graceful curves might be hidden by her gingham and lace.

She heard his footsteps on the flagstone walk and looked around. Her face showed surprise, then she smiled and her blue eyes sparkled. She straightened up, brushed a whisp of hair away from her forehead, and took his hand as he came up.

"Hello, Gil, I didn't know you were coming. I'm sorry I'm such a mess."

He couldn't help smiling. She was a long way from being a mess.

"Let's go into the house," she said, pulling on his hand. "You can talk to Mother while I run upstairs and freshen up."

He held her back. "Martha, let's stay outside and talk. It seems that when we're together, there's always someone else around, your mother or mine. I'd like to be alone with you this time. Let's go over to the swing."

They walked over to the big oak tree on the west side of the house. From one of the branches hung a wooden swing seat that could hold two people. They sat down and began to swing, and Martha started telling him about all the preparations she and her mother were making for the wedding. They had started sewing on her dress and had bought the material for the bridesmaids' dresses. Sometime next week they would order the engraved invitations from a printer in Dallas.

Her cheeks were pink, either from the excitement of talking about the wedding or from exposure to the sun, and her clear blue eyes seemed to dance beneath long lashes. The longer she talked, the more Gil dreaded what he had to do. For a moment he considered not telling her at all, but sending her a letter that she would read after he had gone. But he decided that would be even more cruel.

He took her hand. "Martha, I have to tell you something."

The smile froze on her red lips. "What is it, Gil?"

All at once his mouth was dry. "Tomorrow morning I'm leaving for the frontier. I won't be back for the wedding."

"You . . . won't be back . . . for . . . I don't understand."

He couldn't look at her any longer. He stood up and dug his hands into his pockets. "I just can't marry you, not right now. I'm not ready to settle down. I'd rather take a whipping than tell you this. I know how hard you and your mother have worked, and I'm going to ruin all your plans."

At first she seemed stunned by the news. Then her lip began to tremble and tears rolled down her cheeks. "Oh . . . that's all right." Then she covered her face with both hands and cried.

Gil watched her. It was very strange. All these months he had courted her, he had never felt much affection for her. He had recognized her beauty and talent, and had known that she would make a good wife, because everyone had said so. But now, at the very moment he told her that there would be no wedding, he felt the first stirring of emotion.

She cried for several minutes, then wiped her eyes with a handkerchief. She took a deep breath and clasped her hands in her lap, around the handkerchief. "Why, Gil? Did I do something wrong?"

"No, Lord no! It's hard to explain, Martha. You know about my past. I was raised on the frontier, over in the Palo Pinto country. When I was six years old, the Comanches raided our cabin and killed my mother. My father seemed to fall apart after that and couldn't take care of us children. My brother and sister went to Brenham to live with relatives, and I was taken into the Valkenburg home.

"The Valkenburgs were good to me. I couldn't have asked for better parents. They gave me everything. Maybe they gave me too much. Here I am a man of twenty years, and I haven't done anything with my life. I have energy, I have intelligence, I have ambition, but I've never used them. I've never *had* to use them. If I married you now, I would take over the family property. We'd move into the house with Mother and have everything we're supposed to want.

"Maybe that's all a woman needs to make her happy, but I wouldn't be happy. I would grow old and bitter, because I would know that when I had the opportunity, I didn't go out and test myself against the world. You know, Martha, until last night, I didn't know that I'm a strong man. All these years I've lived in this body and I didn't know what it could do. Oh, I knew that it looked good in the mirror and that I could hang clothes on it. What else can a man do in the Valkenburg mansion?

"Well, last night I learned that I'm strong. I sneaked off to the Keechi Saloon and had a drink with an old frontiersman. While we were there, a man named Trumbull challenged me to an arm-wrestling contest. He was a huge, rough character, and do you know what? *I beat him.* I forced his arm to the table, and I did it without help from anyone. There may be a lot of things I can do with my own wits and ability, and that's what I have to find out. Does that make any sense to you?"

She gave her head a nod. He sat down beside her on the swing. "I have to leave, Martha. I have to go out there and find something. If I didn't, if I stayed here out of duty, you would never care about me. I would make us both miserable. This is the best way for both of us. . . . Tell me what you're thinking."

She pushed the ground with her feet and started the swing. Her eyes were red-rimmed, but she was not crying. "Mother and I have been so busy with all the preparations that I haven't had much time to think about you, Gil. I didn't want to think. Girls aren't supposed to think, you know. Other people decide what is best for us and we're expected to do it. But in my heart, I know you're right."

She turned her eyes on him. "I admire you for doing

what you think is right. You'll be called a scoundrel and the people around town will laugh at my misfortune, but I don't care." She smoothed a wrinkle out of her dress. "I've never loved you. I've never loved anyone. I read poems about love, but no one around here ever talks about it. We have duty and convenience in this town, but I don't know anything about love. Do you? Maybe you have to go to Europe to fall in love. Wouldn't that be fun?"

"Yes."

"I think it would. I hope I fall in love someday." She sighed and gazed off in the distance. Then she stopped the swing with her feet and stood up. "Good-bye, Gil Moreland. I can't promise that I'll wait for you, and maybe you don't want me to. I don't know. A woman has to do what she has to do, even if it's not perfect. But I won't forget you."

She offered her hand. He rose from the swing and pulled her into his arms until he could feel her breasts pressing against his body. She seized the folds of his jacket in her hands and pulled tightly. Mrs. Wynn came out the back door with a basket of laundry in her arms. She stopped on the bottom step and stared at them. She dropped the basket and hurried back inside the house. Gil lifted Martha's chin and kissed her. When he stepped back, her eyes were still closed and her lips glistened with the moisture from him.

"Good-bye, Martha." He backed out the yard gate. She waved with her fingers.

"Will you write?"

"Yes, will you?"

She nodded and smiled a brave smile. He turned and hurried down the street.

5

The sun was just beginning to peep over the tops of the live oak trees when Gil rode Snip up to the livery barn. The air was soft and fragrant with the smells of wet grass and flowers. He climbed down, tied his horse to the hitching rail, and walked inside the dark barn.

"Ben?" Silence. "Ben Woolsey?" No answer. He walked down the center aisle, glancing right and left into the horse stalls. He came to the last stall, peered over the edge, and saw nothing but fresh straw. His heart sank. Ben had left without him. Maybe, when he had sobered up, he had forgotten their talk.

He heard a noise above him and saw a few joints of straw falling through arrows of brilliant sunlight. He looked up to the loft and saw a pair of red, bleary eyes looking back at him.

"Ben, is that you?"

There was a groan. "What's left of me. What do you want?"

"Don't you remember? This is Friday. I'm going with you to Phantom Hill. We're going out West to find adventure."

Ben sat up and brushed the hair out of his face. He had straw in his beard, in his hair, and all over his clothes.

"That's what I need, some adventure," he muttered. "Where's my hat?" He found it and tossed it down to the ground. He reached back and swatted something with his hand. "Good-bye, honey. I don't remember your name, but I never forget a face."

"Bye," said a sleepy voice.

Ben jacked himself up to a crouch and backed down the ladder. Gil helped him down the last four rungs. He was weaving when he had both feet on the ground, and he reeked of stale whiskey. His face was pallid and he had circles under his eyes. He glanced at Gil and managed a smile.

"She'll cry for a couple of days"—he pointed toward the loft—"but she'll get over me." They heard her snoring. He shrugged. "Maybe she won't cry. So you still want to go out West, huh?"

"I'm ready to leave."

He grumbled under his breath. "Taking a green kid out to the frontier sounds like a bad idea to me. Too risky. I don't want to be responsible. But I get all the profits from the trapping, is that what you said?"

"That was our deal."

He rubbed his eyes. "Well, we'll give it a try. But if you get out there and start acting silly, I'll send you home. I'm not used to having a danged kid around."

Gil smiled. "Thanks, Ben."

"You got to follow instructions, lad, and you can start by saddling my horse, that skinny bay down on the end. I need to rest up for the trip."

Gil found the bay, brushed him, and saddled him while Ben sat down and picked straw out of his hair. When they stepped outside, he cringed at the bright light of the sun.

"Can you ride?" Gil asked. Ben was still as drunk as a hoot owl and was having trouble walking.

"Throw me into the saddle. I'll be all right. Head straight west across country. We'll hit Fort Griffin sometime tomorrow."

Gil gave him a boost and threw him into the saddle. Ben tied his reins in a knot, grabbed the saddle horn with both hands, and slumped forward. "God, I had fun," he muttered.

Gil climbed on Snip and led Ben's mount until they were outside of town and away from the barking dogs that had followed them down the street. West of town the frontier began, an endless sea of rolling grassy swells and troughs, dotted here and there with mottes of oak and mesquite and washed with patches of brilliant yellow sunflowers.

Gil filled his lungs with clean air and felt his whole body tingle with excitement. Inside his shirt he could feel the fifty-dollar gold piece slapping against his chest.

The night before, when he had said his last farewell to Mrs. Valkenburg, she had held up a gold chain for him to see. On the chain hung the coin. She had slipped it over his head and said, "This is for luck and security. Don't use it foolishly. It has only one purpose, to buy your life, if that becomes necessary, and to bring you back home to us." Then she had stood on her toes and kissed him on the cheek.

Gil could not imagine that he would ever use the gold piece, since he wore a bulging money belt, but he was glad to have it. A man could always use good luck and gold.

He glanced back at Ben. They were moving along at an easy trot, and Ben was bouncing around in the saddle. "I don't see what keeps you from falling off, Ben."

"Practice, lad."

They rode all morning. By afternoon the sun blazed overhead and the horses were tormented by flies. Ben didn't raise up, complain, or utter a word. Gil brought out some biscuits and dried beef that Pearl had packed into his saddle wallet. He figured that Ben needed sleep more than food.

They traveled about forty miles that day and made camp at a spring of clear water. Ben climbed down, stuck his head into the water, crawled off under a tree, and went to sleep. Gil took care of the horses and watched the sunset. He looked at the stars for a while and fell asleep with his head pillowed on his saddle blanket.

The next morning they got an early start and made good time while it was cool. Ben looked better and said he felt better. Several times during the morning he said, "No more whiskey. I'll never do that again."

Around four in the afternoon they reached Fort Griffin. Gil had never seen the fort and was surprised to find not a fortress but a rather drab collection of wood and stone buildings located on a hill above Clear Fork of the Brazos. The locals called it Government Hill, Ben explained, and it was the home of the Negro troopers of the 6th Cavalry. Gil saw a group of them drilling on the parade ground.

They skirted the east edge of the fort and rode down the hill toward the civilian settlement known as The Flat, a sprawl of shacks and business establishments that began at the foot of Government Hill and extended across the river bottom to Clear Fork. As they rode down the main street, Gil could see that The Flat was a lively and boisterous little town. The long hitching rails in front of the saloons and gambling dens were lined with saddled horses, and laughter and music poured out into the street. The street was congested with traffic: freight wagons drawn by mules and oxen, horse-drawn carriages, and people milling.

The people on the street did not appear to be the same breed of sturdy citizens he had known in Weatherford. Weatherford had its rough element, all right, but here in this raw frontier settlement, the rough-looking characters seemed to be in the majority. But for Gil the biggest shock came from the women he saw. Within the space of five minutes he passed three women; all had painted faces and all were dressed in scanty costumes that would have caused a scandal in Weatherford.

Ben edged his horse over to the left side of the street and stopped in front of a place called the Bee Hive Saloon. He got down, slacked his cinch so that his horse could breathe easier, and threw his reins over the hitching rail. Gil did the same, and they went through the open door into the saloon.

Just inside the door Ben stopped and ran his eyes over the crowd. His hand went to the pistol in his waistband, as though he just wanted to make sure that it was still there before he went any further. Then he walked through the crowd and chose a table near the back. He sat down facing the door.

Gil followed, but in the shuffle, he got cut off by a man and a woman who were dancing. As he threaded his way through the crowd, he passed by the piano and found himself looking into the dark eyes of the woman who was playing. He had the feeling that she had been watching him, but when he smiled and gave her a greeting, she turned away. He made his way to Ben's table. Before he sat down, he looked back and saw that she was watching him again.

"See something you like?" Ben asked.

"I was just looking at the piano player. She's very attractive."

"Yup. That's Vicki."

"You know her?"

Ben shrugged. "Everybody knows Vicki, nobody knows Vicki. She's kind of a celebrity around here. She calls herself Victoria LaRouge, but I don't imagine she was born with that name. Let's order some grub. I'm so hungry that if I put a finger in my mouth, my stomach would jump up and bite it off."

A waiter came to their table and took their order for two steak dinners and beer. The food came twenty minutes later, a big steak, two slices of cold cornbread, and three canned peaches on the side. Ben didn't take the time to cut his meat with knife and fork, but picked up the whole steak in his hands and ripped off chunks with his teeth. When he had devoured the meat, he popped the peaches into his mouth one at a time, then tore into the cornbread. When he had finished, he wiped his hands on his shirt and leaned back, a picture of satisfaction.

Gil was taking his time, cutting his steak into small pieces, just as he would have done at Mrs. Valkenburg's table.

"You go ahead and enjoy your supper," said Ben. "I'm going to prowl around and see if I can find us a room for the night. I'd like to try out a real bed, just to see if I can remember what it feels like. I'll be back in half an hour. And don't get into any fights until we can buy you some artillery. These boys around here are rank."

Gil went on with his supper. The steak was tough and had a slightly tainted flavor—"aged beef," Ben had called it—but he had worked up a big appetite and the imperfections didn't bother him. All at once he became aware of someone standing just behind his left shoulder. He turned around and looked up into the face of Victoria LaRouge.

"Hello," he said. He laid down his fork and stood up, and saw that she was quite small, maybe a foot shorter than his six feet two inches. She wore a full red satin gown that reached to her ankles. It tapered at her tiny waist and was cut low from shoulder to shoulder, revealing the tops of her breasts. Over her shoulders she wore a transparent veil of gauzy red material. LaRouge looked good in red. It must have been her trademark.

"May I sit down?"

"Yes, of course." He held a chair for her and sat down. She said nothing but kept looking at him. It made him uncomfortable, and he didn't know whether he should continue eating or not.

"I haven't seen you in here before," she said at last.

"With so many men coming in and out, how could you be sure you'd remember one face?"

"I'd remember yours."

"I just rode into town an hour ago." Silence. "Could I order you something?"

He had unbuttoned the top button of his shirt at some point earlier in the day, and Vicki saw the gold coin around his neck. She reached out and took it in her hand. "No thanks. I can't stand the food, and I try to avoid liquor. That's a pretty little bauble you're wearing. Gold is my favorite color."

"I would have guessed that red was your favorite."

For the first time, she smiled. "I've been told that I look good in red, but I think I would look better in gold. What's your name?"

"Gil Moreland. And you are Victoria LaRouge."

"Yes, or Vicki the Red for those who can't handle the French."

"You're French?"

"Somewhat. I named myself. In a place like this, you can call yourself anything you want and nobody cares. Half the people in The Flat named themselves."

"Why?"

She withdrew her hand but continued to admire the gold coin. "One never knows, one never asks. Go ahead with your supper. Don't let me disturb you."

He took a bite of steak. She watched him. "I heard you playing the piano. You play well."

"Do you know something about music?"

"I took lessons for a while. I'm no musician, but I admire good music."

"Then you ought to know that what I play is junk."

"But you play it well. I noticed how agile your fingers were. You must have studied technique."

This seemed to amuse her. "You're an observant fellow, aren't you? I'm not used to being around men who can see past the bottom of a whiskey glass. I'll have to watch myself."

"I don't understand what you mean."

"Good." She took a sip from his glass of beer and made a sour face. "Green beer. That's all we can get out here. Last week a keg blew up in the storeroom. Are you passing through or will you be around for a while? I remember your friend, The Beard. He's been in here before."

He told her that they planned to locate at Phantom Hill and spend the winter trapping.

"That's only thirty-five miles down the Fort Concho road," she said. "You'll be coming here for supplies. Next time you're in town, come to the Bee Hive. If you really like good music, I'll play some for you." She got up from her chair.

"Are you leaving already?"

"Your friend just came in the door."

"Ben? That's all right, he'd like to meet you."

"I know he would, but I see his kind every day." She looked down at Gil and patted him on the cheek. "It's your kind that I don't see. Bye now."

She walked away just as Ben came up. He watched her for a moment and sat down. "Vicki was sitting with you? Well, aren't you the honored one! What's your secret?"

"I don't wear cornbread crumbs in my beard."

Ben slapped at his beard and dislodged about half of the crumbs. "You reckon that's it?"

"I wouldn't be surprised." Gil finished his steak, wiped his mouth, and pushed the plate away. "She seems to be a nice lady."

Ben laughed. "Whatever you say. I'll admit that she looks better now that she's off that dope."

"What dope?"

"That opium stuff, painkiller. She was taking it when she got here and was going through it pretty heavy there for a while. Made her look half asleep all the time and she sort of let herself go. They say she's off it now and she's kind of bloomed again. But I wouldn't say she's a nice lady."

"What would you say she was?"

Ben's eyes stopped on the gold piece around Gil's neck. "Is that real gold? I'd advise you to keep it inside your shirt. Somebody around here is liable to cut your neck off and walk away with it. There's some bad people in places like this. Say, I found us a room with a bed. Let's put the horses up at the livery barn, give them a good feed, and go to the hotel. I might even take a bath, you can't ever tell."

Gil followed him through the crowd. At the door, he paused and looked over toward the piano. Vicki was smiling and talking to a man. His back was to the door, so Gil couldn't see his face, but he had wide shoulders and a bull neck.

Out on the street he stopped. Could that have been C. D. Trumbull? He was about to go back for another look when Ben yelled at him to hurry up.

6

The next morning after breakfast, Gil and Ben went shopping for supplies. Ben said that there was a trader at Phantom Hill but that his goods were often of inferior quality and overpriced. He thought they should buy what they could at Griffin and use the Phantom Hill trader only for small items.

He made up an order for flour, sugar, salt, coffee, salt pork, chewing tobacco, soap, and blankets. Then, while the merchant was filling the order, he moved over to the firearms display. He tried out several Sharps and Spencer breechloader carbines, but finally chose a .44 caliber Henry. The magazine under the barrel held fifteen rimfire cartridges and the lever action had a good crisp sound to it. The price was thirty-seven dollars. Then he looked over the sidearms and chose a Colt Navy, also in .44 caliber. He picked out a saddle scabbard for the Henry and a hip holster for the Colt and bought a supply of ammunition for both.

He loaded and primed the Colt and insisted that Gil start wearing it on his hip. He twirled the cylinder and dropped the pistol into Gil's holster. "You never know when you might need this."

Gil felt silly walking around with a pistol on his hip,

when he didn't know how to use it, but he didn't argue. Ben knew what he was doing.

Next, they went to the livery barn and Ben haggled with the owner over a tall dun horse. He bought the dun for fifteen dollars, and they packed all their supplies on his back. Shortly before noon they were ready for the trip to Phantom Hill. As they rode south on their way out of town, they passed by the Bee Hive. Gil looked inside, hoping he might catch one last glimpse of Victoria LaRouge, but he didn't see her.

Up on Government Hill, they struck the military road that ran to Fort Concho. It would lead them to Phantom Hill. They traveled at a leisurely pace, made camp for the night, and pushed on to Phantom Hill the next day, arriving in the late afternoon.

Ben explained that in its prime, Phantom Hill had consisted of several log barracks with stone chimneys, a rock house for the officers, a jail, a commissary, and a powder magazine. But during the Civil War it was surrendered, vacated, and the log buildings burned to the ground. It was never rebuilt and never occupied by soldiers after 1861.

After the war civilians began moving in, first *comanchero* traders from New Mexico, then deserters from both sides of the war, outlaws, hunters, trappers, and cattle drivers who used it as a watering point.

When Gil first saw the place at a distance, it fulfilled every expectation evoked by its name. The sun was settling into a cloud bank that was moving in from the southwest, casting long shadows and bathing the tall prairie grass in an eerie golden light. The old stone chimneys, left suspended and unattached after the barracks had burned, rose in the sky like cenotaphs, while a restless wind moaned through the grass and thunder rumbled in the distance. It was a lonely sight, and Gil could understand why some early explorer had dubbed the place Phantom Hill.

"So this is the frontier," he said. "At last I'm in wild man country."

Ben grunted and looked off toward the dark cloud. "I was hoping you'd forgot the wild man. Say, them clouds are moving this way. We'd better hurry or we're liable to get blowed away."

He spurred his horse into a lope. The packhorse didn't want to move that fast and tried to sull. Ben dallied the lead rope around his saddle horn and dragged the dun out of a slow trot. He threw his head and bucked, while Ben cursed him over his shoulder and hauled him toward Phantom Hill.

The wind was gusting now and it carried the fresh smell of rain. In the distance, they could see a brown cloud of dust rising into the purple rain clouds as yellow spears of lightning stabbed the ground. Gil held onto his hat and rode hard to keep up. Ben galloped into the settlement, scattering chickens and bringing four ugly curs to their feet. The hair on their backs stood straight up, and they went into a fit of barking.

Ben tied his horse in front of a small stone house—the old commissary building, as it turned out—and started unpacking the dun and throwing the supplies inside. "Jerk the saddles!" he yelled over the wind. Gil loosened the cinch on his saddle and dragged it inside. He went back out for Ben's saddle, and the first big drop of rain slapped him on the back of the neck. It was cold and it stung.

The wind was howling now, and overhead the dark clouds boiled. "What do you want to do with the horses?" Gil yelled.

Ben stopped and thought. "We've only got two sets of

hobbles. Hobble yours and the dun. I think mine will stay around."

Gil had just secured the rawhide hobbles around the fetlocks of the dun when a bolt of lightning ripped down from the sky, followed a second later by thunder as loud as a cannon. The dun screamed in fear and lunged forward, knocking Gil to the ground. He grabbed his hat and dived into the house, with the roar of the approaching rain right behind him.

"That was pretty close," said Ben, watching the storm from the door. "We're lucky nobody's moved into my old place. This is where I stayed before."

Gil looked around. It was a sturdy twelve-by-twenty-foot building, with thick stone walls and a wooden ceiling that was covered with mud dauber nests. It seemed a good deal more substantial than some of the other shacks he had seen coming in. "I wonder why nobody moved in."

They heard a buzz not far away. Ben looked toward the sound, drew his pistol, took careful aim, and fired. Flames leaped from the Remington's muzzle, and when the smoke cleared, a headless rattlesnake writhed on the dirt floor. He stuffed the pistol back into his waistband and watched the storm. "Too many spiders, I guess."

"Spiders!"

"And maybe a snake or two. Don't worry about the buzztails. They ain't so bad."

"Unless they bite you."

"That's true, but I'll guarantee you that whiskey and horses kill a lot more folks than snakes do. We'll desnake the place. It'll be all right."

"How do you do that?"

"Run a horsehair rope around the inside wall. They say a rattlesnake won't cross a horsehair rope."

"What do you mean, *'they say'?* Does it work or not?"

"Just in case it ain't true, we'll turn a couple of big bull snakes loose in here. They'll run off the rattlers."

Gil sighed. "I guess we know why nobody moved in."

"I reckon we do." The wind and rain and thunder roared outside. Water was beginning to drip from the ceiling. "Why don't you build us a fire? There's a little fireplace over there in the corner."

"What if I step on a snake?"

"Bite him before he bites you."

"Thanks." Gil groped toward the gloomy corner and started gathering up straw, bits of paper, and sticks that a pack rat had left. He dropped them into the fireplace and was about to reach into his vest pocket for a match when he froze. There was something in the fireplace—something *alive.* In the half darkness, he could see a pair of little round eyes, a beak, and white feathers.

He pushed up to his feet and backed away. "Ben, come here and show me how to start a fire. I've never been very good at it." Ben grumbled and went to the fireplace, digging for a match. Gil stepped back where he could get a good view. "Watch for snakes, Ben."

"Snakes don't bother me." He marched up to the fireplace, knelt down, and struck a match. The chicken exploded, squawking and flapping her wings. Ben was so startled, he cried out and jumped backward. Gil doubled up with laughter. Ben chased the hen around the room, seized her, and threw her outside. Then he shot a glare at Gil. "You ornery little skunk. Light your own fire."

Soon Gil had a blaze going, and by the light of the fire he was able to find some boards and sticks and a thick chinaberry log to add to it. The chinaberry had a good solid core of hard wood, but the outside was punky, and the soft wood gave off smoke that had a foul smell to it. It was a good thing that the chimney drew well in the high wind, or they might have been smoked out.

Ben started unpacking the supplies. He brought out a coal-oil lantern, lit it, and placed it on a crude wooden table over in a corner. Gil started putting the foodstuffs on plank shelves near the hearth, and before long they had nothing to do but sit down and listen to the storm. The roof leaked in several places, but all in all, the old stone commissary was a cozy place to be in bad weather.

Around dark, the rain slacked off and the thunder moved to the southeast. They heard a knock at the door. Ben was sitting at the table, smoking his pipe. He drew his pistol and laid it across his thighs before he told the visitor to come in.

A small, wiry Mexican man pushed the door open and came inside. He wore a wide-brimmed black hat and an oilskin slicker. He had small brown eyes, bronze skin, and several gaps in his smile. Right behind him, and peeking out between his legs, was a little boy of about five years. He had a shock of coal-black hair and big doe eyes.

"Benito?" said the Mexican. "Is it you?"

"Steban!" Ben smiled and went to shake his hand. "And is this little Ruben? How are you, my boy?" Ruben took cover behind his daddy's leg. Ben introduced Gil to Esteban Martinez and insisted that Esteban sit down in the only chair. Ben sat on his bedroll with his back against the wall. Little Ruben was taking no chances with the strangers and stayed behind the chair. Now and then, Gil would see the big black eyes staring at him.

Ben told Esteban where he had been and what he had done, and then Esteban gave the news from Phantom Hill. Charlie Ford and his bunch were hunting buffalo over in the Double Mountain country. Two gamblers from Arkansas had moved in and built a shack on the south edge of town, and they were selling a fair grade of whiskey for fifty cents a glass. Esteban and his brother, Adolfo, were still running sheep down on the Clear Fork meadows, and Celia, Esteban's wife, was pregnant again.

"Must be all this fresh air around here," said Ben with a grin.

Esteban laughed and said, no, he didn't think it was the air.

"Benito, what will you do here? You should buy some sheep."

Ben was a long time in answering. "We're gonna try to run some traps this winter."

Esteban's brows rose. "Traps? But the wild man . . ."

"I know. This was *his* big idea." He jerked his thumb toward Gil. "I got talked into it in a moment of weakness. He's got a good excuse. He's ignert, but I ought to know better. What do you hear from the wild man? You and Celia had him up for supper lately?"

Esteban laughed at this, then the smile vanished. "Celia saw him, it makes two weeks ago. She and this one"—he pointed to little Ruben—"went down to the river to bathe. They took off all the clothes and were naked. Celia was washing the clothes when Ruben said he saw a man. The boy sometimes makes up stories, and Celia did not believe him. She went on washing clothes on the rocks. Then Ruben said, 'Mama, he comes closer. He wears no clothing. He is so big, and look at the hair on his arms.' "

Little Ruben came out from behind the chair, crawled up into his father's lap, and buried his face in Esteban's chest.

"Celia looked up this time, and there was the wild man standing on the other side of the river, maybe thirty steps away. He made no sound, only stared at her. Ruben was not afraid at first and started walking toward him, wading the shallow water. Celia screamed and grabbed the boy's arm, and they ran all the way back home. You know my Celia,

Benito. She is shy and does not run naked through the town without good reason. When I came home at dusk, she was so afraid, so afraid.

"I got my rifle and a lantern and went to the spot. She would not go with me, who could blame her? I found the clothes on the rocks and waded to the other side. I found tracks in the sand, Benito, the tracks of a man wearing no shoes. They were very big. It was the wild man, I am sure of that. Celia will not bathe now unless I am there with a rifle. She cannot forget."

Ben gave a low whistle. "Nobody would forget that."

"And I saw him too, Benito, only two days ago. I was sitting on a hill, watching the sheep below. Maybe I went to sleep. It is hard to stay awake all the time around sheep. I awoke with a strange feeling. Very strange feeling, I cannot describe it only to say strange. *Misterioso.* The sheep were quiet, all was well. I looked around and, Benito, *he was there,* as close as I am to you, so close that I could smell him. He reached out his hand to me. I screamed and ran."

The room was silent except for the popping of the fire. Gil had goose bumps on his arms, and Ben was staring at Esteban with his mouth half open. "Can you describe his smell?"

Esteban shook his head. "All things have a smell, Benito, and I know them all. My nose is good. I know the smell of a sheep, a badger, a deer, a buffalo. A man has a smell, and so does a woman. This was something new to me. It was the smell of a man, but also something else. I cannot describe it, but I will never forget it."

Ben nodded. "You said he reached out to you. What did you think he was going to do? What was the expression on his face? Did you think he was going to hurt you?"

Esteban stared into the fire and didn't reply for a while. He rubbed the back of the boy's head. "No. He could have killed me while I slept. I think he did not want to hurt me. I think he wanted to touch my hair. My hair is curly, not straight like his. He wanted to feel it. The expression on his face was not angry or mean, more like a child. But the yellow eyes, Benito, they struck me with fear. I could not stand to look into them."

"I know. I've seen them too. They would scare the bark off a tree."

"We are all afraid now. I am afraid. Celia wants us to leave this place. She thinks the wild man is a ghost or a devil. Maybe he is. Those yellow eyes are not human."

Esteban had left the door open, and no one had noticed that the hen had walked back inside. All at once, when Ben shifted his position, she squawked and flew outside. Everyone jumped at the sound, then their laughter broke the tension.

"Damned chicken," Ben growled. "If she comes in here one more time, she's gonna end up in my skillet. Steban, try to hang on for a while. You're good neighbors, and I'd sure hate to see you leave. If it'll make you feel any better, this big, gawky kid," he glanced at Gil, "came out here for one reason: he's going to try to catch the wild man. I thought he was crazy—well, I still think he's crazy, but I guess it's time somebody tried to do something."

Esteban's face brightened. "Yes? Oh, that is good news, very good. Celia will be glad to know this. She will like you, I know. She will pray for your success and she will make you very good food. I will help, if I can, and am at your service. We must go. Ruben is sleepy. We are glad to see you back, Benito. Good night."

When they had gone, Ben looked at Gil. "Well, what do you say now?"

"I'm going to ride out first thing in the morning and look for sign."

Ben smirked. "No you're not. You ain't going anywhere to look for anything until I teach you a thing or two. As ignert as you are, we might as well send out little Ruben. So just relax and start paying attention to Perfesser Woolsey."

Perfesser Woolsey yawned. "Let's go to bed."

It was some time in the middle of the night when Gil awoke. He heard something in the room, and he realized that he had been dreaming about the wild man. He felt a chill moving down his spine. He sat up and listened. All at once there was an explosion of noise over on Ben's side of the room.

"Damned chicken!" he squalled. "Get out of here!"

Gil laughed and went back to sleep.

7

It was the third of October. Gil had gone out alone that morning to check the rabbit traps. It was past noon now as he walked through the brush and timber on the Clear Fork bottom. He had four plump cottontail rabbits in his game bag, and he had one more trap to check before he returned to Phantom Hill.

It didn't seem possible that he had been here for two months. The time had passed very quickly, so quickly that he had neglected to write letters to Mrs. Valkenburg and Martha Wynn. But he had been busy. He had spent his days going out into the countryside with Ben Woolsey. Every day he learned something new.

Ben had turned out to be an excellent teacher, but far more demanding than Gil had ever imagined he would be. Ben seemed to have taken it upon himself to teach Gil everything he knew about living on the frontier, and with a lifetime of experience behind him, he knew a great deal. Gil had supposed that he would learn it all in a matter of weeks. Now, with two months of frontier schooling under his belt, he despaired of learning it all in two years—or ever.

What he had never realized was that these rough and illiterate men on the frontier—the hunters and trappers, men like Ben—were in touch with a whole technology based on wilderness living. It was not simple and it was not something that could be mastered in a few weeks. He had acquired a new respect for Ben and the men of his breed. Though many of them could not read or write, though they knew little about manners and social graces, they had become experts in fields that most people in the world didn't even know existed.

Tracking was one of those skills. Before coming to Phantom Hill, Gil had never given much thought to tracks. What was there to think about? A track was a track, and so what? But Ben could look at an animal track for half a minute and tell you the breed of animal, its approximate size and weight, whether it was moving slowly or in a hurry, and the direction in which it was traveling. That kind of knowledge was not important unless you needed food, and then it became very important.

And there were many other skills: marksmanship and the care of weapons, shelter building, fire building, the care and preservation of meats, horsemanship and equine anatomy, camp cookery, snaring and trapping, woodcraft and the use of an ax, butchering, skinning, hide stretching, tanning—and on and on. There seemed to be no end to it, no end to the skills he didn't have and things he didn't know. He was learning, but the learning was painful. Sometimes, when he tried to imitate something Ben had done with the greatest of ease, he felt like a grown man who was learning to walk for the first time.

He stopped and listened. The wind had begun to roar in the tops of the cottonwood trees, sending leaves floating down through the air. Until just minutes ago, the day had been dead still, without even a whisper of wind. This was a north wind and he could feel a chill on his neck. Fall was in the air.

Ben had built the rabbit traps from scrap lumber. Each

trap was a rectangular box about two feet long and eight inches square. It had a sliding door on one end and a trigger system made of small sticks and a piece of string. Cottontails were shy animals and were drawn to holes and dark places. When one entered the box, he went straight to the back end, brushed against the trigger, and caused the trap door to fall. It was an ingenious device, and it worked very well.

Gil had not thought about the wild man in a long time. He had been too busy, and since no one in the community had seen the creature recently, the talk about him had died down. But as he approached the rabbit trap, he stopped and stared, and he knew that the wild man had been here. The box trap lay in pieces on the ground, and the fresh scars on a small hackberry tree nearby told the story: someone had picked up the trap and beaten it into splinters against the tree.

He dropped down to a crouch and studied the sign. He found matted grass and a few bent twigs, but no tracks. He crawled on his hands and knees until he found a patch of bare ground, and there it was in the soft dirt: the perfect print of a human foot. The size and depth of the print indicated that the man who had made it was large. All the reports he had heard about the wild man said that he was large, yet he was still surprised by the size of the track.

He rose and started following the sign toward the south, using the tracking skills that he had learned from Ben. He had gone maybe a hundred feet through the brush when he stopped. He had an odd feeling in the back of his neck, a tingling sensation that began around his hairline and moved down his spine. Esteban had described such a feeling when he told about the day he had seen the wild man.

He turned around slowly. There, fifteen feet behind him, stood a huge, manlike creature, staring at him with the yellow eyes of a wolf. His hair was long, black, and coarse, and it fell across his shoulders and hung to his chest. Coils of black hair covered his entire body. There was something about his face that was terrifying. Looking at it, Gil saw the familiar features of a man—eyes, nose, mouth—molded into the immobile expression of an animal.

For a moment he was giddy with fear. He could hear the rapid beating of his heart and the blood rushing past his eardrums. Sweat popped out on his face, yet he felt cold. And that feeling in the back of his neck persisted, as though ants were crawling under his skin. All at once he realized that his right hand had closed around the butt of his pistol.

They stared at each other for several minutes. Neither moved. The wild man's gaze came as straight as the path of an arrow. He didn't move his eyes nor did he blink them. Animals were able to do that. Humans blinked. Gil relaxed his hand and released his grip on the pistol. He licked his lips, which had become dry, and took a slow, steady breath.

"What is your name? *Como se llama usted?* My name is Gil. Don't be afraid of me, I'm not going to hurt you." The wild man did not respond. There was absolutely no expression on his face, no line or wrinkle or movement of skin to indicate what might be going through his mind.

Gil moved toward him. He took one slow step and waited to see what would happen, then another and another. The wild man stared at him, as motionless as a slab of rock. Gil kept walking. When he was within five feet of the creature, he stopped. The face was still a blank, but he could see that the wild man's body had tightened. His big arms were quivering ever so slightly. At this close distance Gil caught the scent. There was something human and familiar about it, perhaps the pickled smell of sweat. But, as Esteban had noted, there was more, a strange musky odor that was hard to identify.

Gil reached out his hand. A tremor passed through the wild man's body and he took a step backward. "I'm not going to hurt you," Gil said in a soft voice. "Don't be afraid of me. I want to know who you are. Do you know? Can you understand anything I'm saying? Your parents must have been humans. Who were they, where did they come from? Were they Indians?"

In the blink of an eye the wild man turned and ran into the timber. Gil was amazed that a man so large could move so quickly. "Wait! Don't run away!" He threw down his game bag and started running after him, watching the ground ahead for sign. He had gone about a hundred yards when, out of the corner of his eye, he caught a glimpse of an arm coming at his face. It struck him above the right eye, and the blow was delivered with such force that it lifted him off his feet and threw him on his back. Had he not seen the arm with his own eyes, he would have thought that he had been hit with a club.

A shower of color sprayed over the darkness behind his eyes, and for an instant he thought that he would slip into unconsciousness. Then he felt the crushing weight of the wild man on his midsection and a pair of powerful hands closing around his throat. He realized that if he passed out, he might never awaken. He forced his eyes open and looked into the face of the man-animal. The lips were curled back, exposing clenched teeth, and there was a deadly rage burning in those yellow eyes.

Gil summoned every ounce of strength in his body and fought back. The wild man's hands were choking off his wind. He couldn't breathe, and he couldn't break the powerful grip. Blood from his cut clouded his vision, and he could feel the warm trickle running down his neck. He gasped for air and thrashed. There was so much pressure behind his face now that he feared his eyes would pop out of his head. He aimed a blow at the wild man's face, but it didn't reach the mark. He felt darkness closing in on him. He had only thirty seconds left, maybe less.

Then he saw a weakness. He reached out and seized the wild man's long hair and pulled on it with all his strength. The wild man screamed in pain and rolled away. Gil leaped to his feet and rammed his shoulder into the wild man's back. His head snapped back, he grunted like an animal, and went sprawling to the ground. They rolled through the brush, snapping branches and throwing up dirt. Each man was kicking and clawing. Gil's blood was on both of them now, in streaks and spots.

Gil began to notice a dull pain in his right hand. A moment later he saw that the wild man had bitten off his little finger at the second joint. It hung by a single flap of skin. He made a fist of that same hand and drove it straight into the yellow eyes. Flesh and bone squished, and the wild man went reeling backward into the brush. In an instant, he was on his feet again. He came in a crouch, his big hands bent into claws. Blood dripped from his nose.

Gil panted for breath, but he wasn't tired. He seemed to be intoxicated by the sudden release of power in his body. He wanted more.

"Come on," he taunted. "How do you like the taste of your own blood?"

The wild man sprang at him, and Gil felt the claws rake a path down the side of his face. He landed a solid punch to the gut, but it had no effect. The wild man was as hard as lumber. They grappled, went to the ground, rolled, and came back up. Gil kept going back to the wild man's weak spot, his long hair.

As the battle raged on, he sensed that he was gaining the upper hand. The wild man seemed to be wearing down. Gil waited for an opportunity to land another punch to the face, but he didn't get the chance. The wild man got there first.

It was a slap made with an open hand. It came out of nowhere, and it knocked Gil senseless to the ground. Had the wild man delivered such a blow with a hard fist, it might have broken Gil's skull. He braced himself for another attack, but when he looked up, he saw the wild man staggering away. His face was battered and smeared with blood.

"Wait!" Gil cried. The wild man stopped and glared at him with his wolf eyes. Gil pointed a finger at him. "I'll get you. Do you understand? I'll get you, I don't care how long it takes."

The wild man growled and gave his head a shake. He vanished into the brush.

Gil slumped back to the ground and felt the pistol digging into his side. He had forgotten about the pistol, but he hadn't needed it anyway. He had fought the wild man to a draw, hand-to-hand, strength against strength, and the wild man knew he had been in a dog fight. Gil felt a rush of exhilaration, but it didn't last long as he began to feel the effects of the struggle. His arms and legs quivered. His face throbbed and so did his finger.

He held up his right hand. It was covered with dried blood, and fresh red blood oozed from the stump that had been his little finger. The end of it still dangled from a piece of skin. He bit it off and spit it out on the ground.

He pushed himself up and staggered against a tree. He had taken a worse beating than he had thought. He felt dizzy and his vision was foggy. He looked at the scene of the struggle. The ground and brush in a twenty-foot circle lay torn and broken, as though two powerful beasts had fought here. He picked his hat off the ground, found his bearings from the sun, and started back to Phantom Hill. He remembered that he had left his game bag, but he lacked the strength to go find it. He would be doing well to make it back to the settlement.

Ben had left a chair out in front of the stone house that morning, and Gil fell into it and let his head drop back against the wall. Another ten feet and he could have had water, a damp cloth for his forehead, a rag for his finger, and a pallet to lie on. But he had gone as far as he could go, and ten more steps were ten steps too many. He sat there with his arms dangling at his sides, waiting for his strength to return and for the throbbing to stop.

Ben came walking up. He had spent the morning cutting strips of venison and hanging them on racks to dry. He was preoccupied with his own thoughts and did not look at Gil very closely at first. Then he stopped.

"My God, what happened to you!"

Gil tried to smile. "I introduced myself to the wild man."

"You *what?*"

"Ben, I fought him. I didn't lose. I'm as strong as he is."

Ben licked his lips. "How bad are you hurt?"

"I don't know. Just what you see, I think. Tired, mostly."

"Stand up and look at yourself."

Gil pushed himself up out of the chair. Ben took his arm and helped him. He ran his eyes over his body. His shirt had been torn to shreds, and the left leg of his pants had been ripped. He had deep claw marks on his chest and abdomen and down both arms, teeth prints on both arms, and bruises, blood spots, grass stains, and smudges of dirt everywhere.

Ben's face was very solemn. "If you didn't lose the fight, what does *he* look like? Did you kill him?"

"No, but I got in some good licks. He quit, he didn't want any more." Gil eased back into the chair and told the whole story. "And Ben, just before he left, I said, 'I'm going to get you.' I think he knew what I said, maybe not the exact words, but he understood. He shook his head. That's a universal response, isn't it? It's common to all the languages I know about."

Ben picked up Gil's right hand and looked at the bloody stump. "What happened here?"

"I'm not sure, but I guess he bit my finger off."

Ben dropped the hand. "Get yourself cleaned up. We're going to Griffin."

"Why?"

"You need a doctor, before your whole arm rots off." Ben explained that one of the most dangerous bites in all creation was the bite of a human. "The mouth of a man is filthy, partly because we eat so much meat and partly because we're just filthy animals. A human bite doesn't look bad at first, but just wait a few days. It'll go to blood poison and then to gangrene. I've seen it happen, and it ain't pretty."

Gil didn't want to make the long trip to the fort. He was too tired and he wanted to sleep. But Ben convinced him that it was necessary, and Ben went out to saddle the horses.

Gil went inside and poured some water in a pan. The white hen was sitting in the wooden box Ben had made for her. After all the raging and threatening he had done, he had lacked the will to wring the chicken's neck. Instead, he had built her a nest and moved her inside. She left droppings all over the floor, and the place had the smell of a chicken house. Gil didn't have the heart to make an issue of it, since old Ben had grown so fond of her.

He tore off what remained of his clothes and washed his wounds with water and hard lye soap, which burned like fire. An hour later, they started out for Fort Griffin.

8

Dr. Gibson, the head surgeon at Fort Griffin, was a small man with unhappy eyes. He ordered Gil to strip and sit on the examining table.

He studied the scratches on Gil's arms and chest, then pulled his head down so that he could examine the cut over his right eye. He snatched Gil's right hand and turned it around. He dropped the hand and went to a cabinet in the corner. He walked with a limp.

Dr. Gibson must have been sour on the world, Gil decided, because he handled his patients with a rough, jerky touch, the way a man would handle meat.

He returned, smelling of carbolic acid and holding a needle and thread. "Lie down."

"Are you going to . . ."

"Lie down." Dr. Gibson turned to Ben. "Hold his arms. I don't want him thrashing."

"I don't think he'll thrash."

The doctor gave a little sigh and stepped out into the hall. He called someone and a moment later two burly Negro soldiers came in. "Hold his arms while I put in these sutures."

Gil sat up. "Get them out of here. I don't need anyone to hold me down. Get on with it."

The doctor glared at him. "You people drink yourselves into a stupor, get into a brawl over nothing, and come in here expecting me to sew you back together. I'm not going to wrestle with you to put in these sutures."

"Fine. Get those goons out of here and I'll take care of myself."

The doctor dismissed the soldiers with a jerk of his head. "Lie down."

Gil lay back on the table. "And just for your information, Doctor, I didn't get all this in a drunken brawl."

Dr. Gibson wasn't interested in the details. He swabbed the cut as though he were mopping a floor and went to work with his needle and thread. Either Gil's hide was very thick or the needle was dull, because the doctor had trouble penetrating the skin. He poked and gouged and finally bullied it through. It took ten stitches to close the wound on his forehead, and the stitching hurt a good deal worse than the original injury. Gil had to clamp his jaws together to keep from crying out, but he didn't move.

When Gibson finished closing this wound, he went to work on Gil's finger. "Have you had chills or sweats with this?" Gil said no. "Have you noticed a rapid pulse?" Gil shook his head. "You were smart to come in when you did. In another day or two, it could have gone to septicemia. What happened?"

Gil glanced at Ben. He shrugged. "I was wrestling with a fellow and he accidentally bit it off. But it wasn't a drunken brawl."

Gibson smirked. "I see. I'm going to wash it out with antiseptic. It might sting."

He washed the wound out with carbolic acid and closed it with three neat sutures. Then he swabbed the whole finger with a strong solution of iodine. The carbolic acid and iodine sent waves of fire up Gil's arm, but he didn't utter a sound. Gibson dressed the stump with a gauze bandage and washed his hands.

"What sort of fellow was this who bit off your finger—accidentally, of course?" Gil told him about the wild man and noticed that he listened with keen interest. When he had finished the story, Gibson asked, "Is that true? I've heard rumors about this creature, but I never believed them. I don't suppose you would have any reason to lie about it."

"No, sir, I don't."

Gibson lit a small cigar and inhaled the smoke. "That's fascinating. If you manage to capture this wild man, and if you're ever around the fort, I wish you'd bring him in and let me examine him. I have a passing interest in such things. I'd like to know more about him."

Gil said that he would, and Gibson's manner became businesslike again, though he was a bit more friendly now. "You have the beginnings of a septicemia, blood poisoning. I hope we caught it in time. Soak the finger three or four times a day in hot salts, as hot as you can stand. Come back in two days and let me look at it again. Will you be staying in The Flat?" Ben said yes. "Then let me give you some advice. The women at the Place of Beautiful Sin are poisonous. The women at Lottie's are so-so. The Bee Hive is a fairly clean place."

Outside, Ben and Gil walked down Government Hill toward The Flat. "Ben, is Victoria LaRouge a prostitute?"

Ben shot him an amused glance. "What do you think?"

"I don't know. You're the man of the world. That's why I asked you."

"Of course she is. She don't walk the streets or work for a house, but she's in business."

"But she seemed so nice, and she plays the piano very well."

"She was nice to you because you look like a man with money. You ever had a woman before?"

"A few times."

"Good. I'd hate for you to get silly and fall in love. I'd be embarrassed. People might say I hadn't schooled you very good. Vicki's broken a lot of hearts. You might keep that in mind."

They walked to the bottom of the hill and started down the main street of The Flat. It was six o'clock in the evening, and the saloons were already jumping with music and laughter.

"Tell you what let's do," said Ben. "You go your way and I'll go mine. I'll meet you at the Bee Hive at noon on Wednesday. We'll take you to see the doc and head out for Phantom Hill. Soak that finger, like he said, and don't get yourself shot over a woman. There ain't a woman here that's worth it. See you around."

He walked on down the street, looking into the saloons and gambling halls, and disappeared into the evening crowd. Gil went into the Bee Hive.

She was at the piano again, dressed in red. She played a slow, mournful song that had come out of the Civil War years, and she seemed completely absorbed in watching her fingers move over the keys. Tonight she had a red rose behind one ear. Gil walked over to the piano and stood there for several minutes. At last her dark eyes came up.

"Hello, Vicki. Do you remember me?"

She looked him over, and he knew that she didn't remember him. "Sure, but you'll have to tell me your name again."

He brought the fifty dollar gold piece out of his shirt and held it up. "Now do you remember me?"

The corners of her mouth turned up in a smile, and she let her eyelids droop low over her eyes. "The fellow who likes music. Sure. But you'll still have to help me with the name."

"Gil Moreland."

"That's right. Gil Moreland. You were in here with The Beard—your friend, that is. He ate like a starved dog."

Gil laughed. "That's Ben, all right. You said you would play me some good music when I came back."

"Did I?" She finished the song, but instead of ending it with a resolution of the chords, she left the musical line hanging on an unresolved, dissonant chord. Nobody in the saloon noticed or cared. "I hope I can remember some good music. There's no demand for it here." She stood up, took the rose from behind her ear, and pushed it into the neck of his shirt, so that it rested on the gold chain. "Shall we go to my place or yours?"

"I don't have a place."

"Neither do I," she said in an offhand manner, "but I have a house. Shall we go?"

She threw a white shawl over one shoulder and walked toward the back of the saloon. As she went past the bar, she picked up a full bottle of whiskey and spoke to the bartender. "See you around, Eddie." Eddie looked Gil over from top to bottom before he went back to his work.

They went out the back door and into a dark alley. Vicki walked in a long, slow, swinging stride and looked up at the evening sky. She seemed distant, hardly aware that he was there beside her. They had gone several blocks before she looked at him again.

"What did you get into?"

"I beg your pardon?"

She pointed to his face and hand. "You look like you fell into a buzz saw. No wonder I couldn't remember your face. You were pretty the last time I saw you."

"I'll tell you about it later. It's kind of a strange story."

"Uh-oh."

They came to a small white frame house that stood off by itself on the edge of town. Behind the house was a wooded creek, and on the other three sides it was surrounded by empty pastures. Vicki slid a key into the lock and pushed open the door. But instead of going in, she leaned her elbow on the door jamb and looked at him.

"I can wait on your story, friend, but let's get something straight before we go inside. I was entertaining a man once. He was a nice fellow, handsome like you, but he liked to drink, and when he drank he liked to punch women around. You see this?" She pointed to a thin scar on her right cheek. She had disguised it with makeup, but it was still visible. "He punched me around and had a big time of it. Later, he had to go to the hospital."

"What happened?"

"He got into some hot bacon grease. So if you're a puncher, maybe you'd better run along." She pierced him with her gaze. "I don't like punchers."

"Neither do I. Let's go in."

She flipped her shawl so that it wound around his neck. She smiled at him and gave the shawl a tug. They went inside and she lit a kerosene lamp. As she turned up the wick, Gil looked around the house. The furnishings were simple but clean and neat. The piano stood over on the south wall. It had been cared for, and the black finish was polished to a high gloss. Vicki brought two glasses out of the kitchen. She poured Gil half a glass of whiskey and barely covered the bottom of hers. She set her glass on a table near the piano and opened a cedar chest. The aroma of cedar filled the room. She brought out a sheaf of music and sat down on a velvet-covered stool at the piano.

"Any requests?" she asked.

"No. Just play."

He sat down in a deep upholstered chair, crossed his legs, and listened. The title on the first page of the music was "E Minor Piano Concerto." She began playing, and Gil knew that he had guessed right: she was an accomplished pianist. Her fingers seemed to float over the keys, and her whole body swayed with the haunting melody. The music expressed longing and melancholia, as though it had been composed on the top of a mountain with the wind moaning in the tops of tall pines. When she came to the end of the piece, her body seemed to fall into the last chord, and she did not move until the notes had died away.

She had played the entire piece without turning past the first page of the music.

She straightened her back, took a deep breath, and reached for her glass. She threw the liquor down in one gulp. "Well, there you are. Good music."

"Vicki, that was beautiful."

She spun around on the stool, and just for a moment, her eyes were soft and vulnerable and filled with childish delight. "Really? You liked it? Do you know the composer?"

"Liszt?"

"Oh no, no! He hammers and bangs and plays with his feet. I can't play his things. Chopin. He composed in Paris and died in forty-nine. No one has come along to replace him. He was a god."

"Play some more, please."

She played for an hour without stopping or looking up, and she played entirely from memory. Gil sat glued to his chair, listening and watching her hands flow over the keys. He hardly moved.

She closed the piano and turned the stool around. "That's enough. Even great music gets tiresome after a while. So. Shall we get on with the next movement?"

"Let's talk a while."

This amused her. "You're a strange fellow, Gil Moreland."

"Where did you learn to play like that?"

She straightened an earring. "Do you want the short version or the long one?" He said the long one. "Oh my, I haven't told the long version in many a moon. Most of the people around here aren't interested, but you might be. All right. As life stories go, it's not bad.

"I was born and raised in New Orleans, good French breeding with just a whisper of English scandal. A soldier, they say. My father was a merchant on the river and we were wealthy. Mother died when I was born. I was Father's little princess and I could do anything I wanted. All he asked was that I learn to play the piano. On that he was very strict. He knew that I was gifted, and when I was seventeen, he sent me to Boston to study under a master.

"He was a horrible German, but probably the most brilliant pianist in America at that time. His music could bring tears from a tombstone. I was an ignorant girl and I didn't know that all musicians are monsters. He seduced me—or I seduced him; I don't suppose it matters—and I married him. I had heard all the romantic tales about Liszt and Countess d'Agoult, Chopin and Sand, and I had visions of a union of art and love.

"It wasn't that way. Rainer hated me for my talent and tried to destroy me. He very nearly did. After one of our fights I took a large dose of laudanum, tincture of opium. I thought it would kill me, but I was mistaken. It merely made me feel better, and I started taking it on a regular basis. With the laudanum, I could stand to live with the German.

"Before long, I was addicted. I couldn't give it up. When Rainer found out what was going on, he flew into a righteous rage—no one can do it better than the Germans—and threw me out into the street. I had nothing but the clothes on my back. I began playing in saloons and . . . doing other things. I went to New York, Philadelphia, then to St. Louis. I wanted to go home. I needed help. I caught one of my father's boats to New Orleans . . . are you sure you want to hear all this?"

"Yes, I do. Please go on."

"Father had remarried and things had changed. I wasn't the little princess any more. The new woman and I didn't get along. She thought I would bring disgrace to the house, so Father asked me to leave. I guess he couldn't help it, but I've never forgiven him for that. He gave me five hundred dollars and told me to leave my home. I took a steamship to Indianola, Texas, and worked my way north and west. I washed up on this beach two years ago, and I'm still here. But I'm going to get out."

"Are you still addicted?"

She looked away. "No. I was until four months ago. The reason I stayed here so long was that I had a contact at the fort, a doctor who kept me supplied with laudanum. Oddly enough, he was addicted too. We found each other and sank together."

"His name wasn't Gibson, was it?"

"Why, yes, it was. Dear old Norman Gibson. Do you know him?"

"He stitched me up this afternoon."

She shrugged. "He helps some people. He didn't help me much. He wanted favors."

"How did you break the addiction?"

She rose and walked to the window. "You can only sink so low, and then you either die or try something better. I guess I wasn't ready to die, so I fought it." She turned around and there was fire in her eyes. "All alone. I had no help. Everyone in this piece of hell wanted me to stay in the gutter with them.

"I suffered. I was sweating and vomiting and gripped by these horrible cramps. No one brought me food. No one gave me water or wiped my brow with a cool towel. No one held my hand or told me to be courageous. Do you know what they did?"

She thrust out her arm and pointed to the door. "They banged on my door at all hours of the night and demanded *sex.* And I gave it to them and I took their money and I cried with pain and vomited in the bed. And do you know what? They didn't know the difference. *They didn't know the difference!*" She turned away. "You shouldn't have asked. No, it's not your fault. I shouldn't have talked. Never talk about yourself, Victoria, because the customers don't want to hear. It's bad for business." She straightened her back and took a deep breath. When she turned to him, that same hard set of the eyes had returned. "Come on, my good man, I'll make it up to you. I'm good. We'll have lots of fun, and you can forget everything I've said." She reached behind her dress and started pulling buttons.

"Don't, Vicki."

Her arms dropped to her sides. "I had you for a while. I could see the hunger in those pretty blue eyes, and I blew it all away with my big mouth and sad story. Damn it. Damn it!" She grabbed the bottle and threw a splash of whiskey into her glass. She drained it in one gulp, then glared at him. "Well? Go home. I've got work to do and you're wasting my time."

"Sit down. I want to talk to you."

She set her glass down on the table and went to the same cedar chest that had held the music. She came out holding a two-shot Derringer. "I don't have time to sit down and talk. Maybe you don't understand. I'm a working girl. I'm saving my money so that I can crawl out of this pit. I don't make money talking. Get out."

There was no trembling in the hand that held the pistol, and there was no indecision in her eyes.

"Sit down, Vicki, and put away your artillery. I'll pay for your time."

"Put the money on the table."

"How much?"

She cut her eyes from side to side. "Five dollars."

"The going rate is two."

"All right, two."

He counted out fifty dollars in ten-dollar gold pieces and laid them on the table. "That's for the beautiful music." Her gaze went to the gold and back to him. He smiled. "Go ahead, take it. I'm buying you for the next two days."

Still holding the pistol on him, she reached out, scooped up the coins, and dropped them into her bosom. She eased into a chair that was a safe distance away from him and laid the pistol in her lap. Not once did she take her eyes off him.

"I've met all kinds," she said, "but never one like you. I don't understand."

"Maybe you're trying to make it too complicated. I'm just what I appear to be."

She shook her head. "It doesn't work that way, not on my side of the street. What do you want?"

He laughed. "I want to hear your music, talk to you, enjoy your company, and sleep on your floor because I don't have a room. That's all I want."

"You're a charming devil. I almost believe you—but not quite. This pistol stays in my lap, and I promise that it's loaded."

All at once they heard someone coming up the steps, then pounding at the door. "Open up!" yelled a man with a deep voice. "I know you're in there! Open the door or I'll break it down!"

Vicki's face went white. "Oh, God," she murmured, "it's Trumbull."

9

Gil stared at her. "C. D. Trumbull?"

"Yes. I'll try to get rid of him. He's drunk, I can tell."

She went to the door and opened it a crack. Gil noticed that she had left the pistol on the table, which he thought was strange.

"Trumbull, go away, I'm busy now."

"Yeah, they said you was. Get *un*busy."

"You're drunk. Go away. I'll talk to you later."

"Don't tell me what to do, woman. You're *mine,* and don't you forget it. Let me in."

"Please go away."

"I'm coming in. Tell your little boyfriend . . ."

Gil pushed Vicki aside and stuck the barrel of his Colt against Trumbull's chest, just as he was stepping in the door. "I'm her little boyfriend. What was it you wanted to tell me?"

Trumbull's little black eyes glistened beneath his shaggy brows. He looked at Gil with a smirk. "Well! It's the lad from Weatherford. What are you doing out here among the men? I didn't figger you was old enough to be whoring around."

"Now you know. Was there anything else you wanted to say?"

Trumbull dropped his smile and narrowed his eyes. "Yeah. The Red belongs to me. You best run along and play."

Gil cocked the hammer on the Colt. "She's busy right now. Come back in two days."

"All right, sonny boy," Trumbull murmured. "You got the goods this time, but you'd better watch your step from now on. Trumbull don't forget." He whirled around and disappeared into the night.

Gil closed the door and bolted it. He carried the lamp into the bedroom, just in case Trumbull tried to shoot through a window. Vicki was sitting in a chair, staring at the floor. Her face was as pale as chalk.

"How did you get mixed up with that character?"

"I don't know. Just bad luck." Her eyes came up. "Thanks. Will you let me earn my money?"

"You already have. You played beautiful music."

"You know what I mean."

"I know what you mean, but no thanks, not now."

"Is something wrong with me?" He shook his head. "Then is something wrong with *you?"*

He laughed. "No. It just doesn't seem right."

She shrugged. "Well, if you're satisfied, that's all a girl can do. But I don't understand you."

Later, when Gil was pulling off his boots and getting ready to bed down on the floor, Vicki appeared at her door. She was wearing a thin cotton nightgown. With the lamp light behind her, Gil could see the outline of her body, a tiny waist that flowed into broad, firm hips. His heart pounded. She looked at him with eyes that were pretty on the surface but cool and hard within. A smile tugged at one side of her mouth. She seemed to be mocking him. She arched one brow, blew him a kiss, and disappeared. She left the door open.

He lay awake for a long time, thinking that any minute he would get up and go to her. But every time his imagination formed a picture of her face, he saw the hard eyes and the brittle smile. He had a feeling that, if he went to her, he would be disappointed. Then he heard a snore come from her room, and he let that settle the matter for him. It was just as well.

The next morning he awoke to the smells of coffee and bacon. He wandered into the kitchen. Vicki stood over a small wood cook stove, watching bacon sizzle in a big cast-iron skillet. She wore a red housecoat that reached to her ankles. She had taken her hair down. It reached past her shoulders and it was frizzy and oily near the ends. In the bright morning sunlight, he could see that she had not removed her makeup from the night before.

Her eyes came up from the stove and went straight to the gold piece around his neck. "Good morning."

He told her good morning and pointed to the skillet. "Are you preparing that hot grease for me?"

She gave him a sly grin. "You never know, mister. Depends on how you act."

"Is the coffee ready?"

"It's ready. Get it yourself."

He poured a cup of coffee, dragged a chair to the edge of the kitchen, and sat down to watch her. He began to notice that she was sending dark looks in his direction. "What's the matter, Victoria, am I bothering you?"

She shook her head and turned the bacon. "Well, maybe you are. I'm not used to having a man around in the morning. I can take you boys at night, but the morning is my private time."

"Am I one of the boys now?"

"You're not one of the girls."

"You don't care much for men, do you?"

She poked at the bacon and didn't answer for a long time. "Maybe not. But you know what? I'm around them all the time. I hardly ever see the other girls around here, just pass them on the street now and then. My father used to say that you should never sympathize with people who complain about their lot in life, because most people are doing exactly what they want to do. So who knows?"

"I'll leave if you want me to."

"Don't worry about it. I can stand it for two days. Besides, you're paid up. This is easy money. For fifty dollars you can watch me all you want." She lifted the bacon out and dropped it on a plate. "You never did tell me your story. How did you get all beat up?"

While she fried the eggs, he told her about his encounter with the wild man. She put their plates on the table and they sat down to eat. When he came to the end of the story, she was eating. She had shown almost no reaction.

"Well?" he said. He noticed that she held her fork in the same way she might have held a trowel, gripping it in a tight fist.

"Well what? What do you want me to say? If it's true, it's quite a story."

"What would make you think it's not true?"

She dropped her fork and leaned on her elbows across the table. "Listen, if I believed every man who comes in this place, I'd be nuts. They're all rich, they're all famous, they're all in love with me, they're all coming back next week to save me from this soiled life. And they're all liars. I don't know why, but when a man walks in that door, he starts telling lies. Listening to them—and not believing them—is part of the business."

"You keep lumping me in with villains like Trumbull. Can't you see any differences?"

"A horse is a horse, whether he's black or white."

"But the difference between one horse and another is what's up here." He tapped himself on the temple. "Some are honest and some are counterfeit. You see the very worst kind of men, and you see them when they're *at* their worst. That's not the whole picture. What about Chopin? Do you think he was the same as Trumbull? He wasn't, and neither am I."

She took the last bite of egg and washed it down with coffee. "All right. You're different, you're a nice fellow, and I can't see any reason why you would lie about the wild man. I'll believe you. You're wearing a ring. Are you married?"

"It was my mother's. She gave it to me before she died."

Vicki grabbed his hand and looked at the ring. "It's nice. I like it. May I have it?" She batted her eyes and gave him a little girl's smile. When he shook his head, she shrugged and dropped his hand. "You never know until you ask. So what will you do with this wild man if you catch him?"

He leaned back in his chair and crossed his arms over his chest. "Well . . . I haven't thought much about that. I'll teach him language. Maybe I'll teach him to read. Maybe I'll teach him to play Chopin on the piano."

"And what if he doesn't want to learn all those wonderful things?"

"He will. Given a clear choice between ignorance and enlightenment, I think most people would choose to be enlightened."

She started laughing and couldn't stop. There was a harsh, jagged quality to her laughter, and it irritated him.

"What's so funny?"

"Lord, you're so young! If you lived in The Flat for one month, you could never say something like that. You know what I think? I think people *love* ignorance and stupidity and ugliness, and they would choose it every time over what you call enlightenment. People live in this piece of hell because they want to be ugly."

"What about you?" The question just popped out of his mouth, and he could see that it caught her off guard.

"I'm going to leave. I told you that. I'm saving my money."

"I gave you fifty dollars last night. That could take you five hundred miles in any direction."

Her eyes disappeared behind her cup. "When I get three hundred dollars saved, I'll leave."

"How much have you saved?"

"That's none of your business." She got up and started clearing the table.

While she washed the dishes, he soaked his finger in hot salts. It seemed to be healing and there were no signs of blood poisoning.

In the afternoon they went for a walk down the wooded creek behind her house and to the river. As they walked through the sand, he took her hand. She gave him an amused look but didn't try to pull away. But her hand was cool and limp, and after a while he let it go.

They ate supper at the Bee Hive. Gil kept an eye out for Trumbull but didn't see him. After the meal, they walked back to her house and she played the piano for him. But it was different this time. She didn't play with the same intensity or passion she had shown the night before. She seemed restless and flat and irritable. He didn't understand this, and when he asked her about it, she said she had a headache. She went to bed early, and this time she closed the door.

As he lay on the floor, looking into the darkness, he began to understand that she was tired of him. She missed the noise and excitement of the Bee Hive. In her own cryptic fashion, maybe she had explained herself to him: "Most people are doing what they want to do."

10

Winter was coming. Gil could feel it in the crisp morning air and see it in the way the shadows fell in the late afternoon. It was the middle of November, and he still hadn't captured the wild man.

He got down off his horse, hobbled him, and let him graze on the tall, dry grass along the floodplain of the Clear Fork bottom. He went over to a big cottonwood tree and sat down, leaning his back against the trunk, and started eating his lunch. It consisted of two of Celia Martinez's cornmeal tortillas, some jerked venison, a handful of dried peaches, and a canteen of water. From where he sat he could look up and see a flight of geese cutting across the blue-gray sky. A moment later he heard their honking. It was a mournful sound, the only sound on this breathless autumn day.

A week had passed since the two trappers had come around to talk. Marlow and Schafer were their names. They were rough, bearded men from the hill country around Fredericksburg. They had come to the Clear Fork country to trap, and they planned to stay the winter.

They were silent men who spent most of their time alone and had little to say, and it didn't take them long to come to the point. They wanted to know if Ben had decided on a territory for his trapping. He hadn't, but said he would give it some thought. Marlow and Schafer nodded their heads at this and fell silent. It appeared they had finished their business, yet they didn't leave.

Then Marlow started talking. He was the spokesman for the two. "We've heard about this wild man. We've heard he robs traps. We've heard that you," he looked at Gil, "came out here to catch him alive. We don't want no trouble, but we'll start trapping around December 15, after the first hard frost. If the wild man is still running loose, and if he bothers our traps, we're gonna kill him. We don't want no hard feelings about it."

After they left, Gil talked to Ben. "I can't imagine anyone just shooting him down like a dog."

"You can't? I can imagine it real easy, and you could too if your livelihood was at stake."

"But he's human, and he's unarmed. If you shot him, it would be cold-blooded murder."

"That's what it would be, all right," Ben nodded. "Besides love, the best reason for murder is money. Marlow and Schafer ain't here for the good climate, lad, they're here to make money on pelts. That's what I'm here for too, in case you forgot."

This was the first Ben had said about the matter, but apparently he had been thinking about it. "Ben, you know I've tried. I've been going out every day. I've found his sign, I know he's out there, but I just haven't been able to catch him."

"Yup, and time's running out. In another month it'll be time to put out the traps. What do you expect us to do, sit around all winter until the pelts lose their prime?"

"Have *you* thought about shooting the wild man?"

"Sure, I've thought about it. It's the only sensible thing to do. It would save us all a lot of trouble."

"Is that what you want us to do?"

"I said I'd *thought* about it. I said it was the sensible thing to do. I didn't say I could do it." He pointed to the chicken roosting at the foot of his bed. "Look at that. I should have killed that fool the second day we were here, but I didn't have the heart to do it. Now she's taking the place over. Any day now, I expect her to tell *me* to move out. I must be getting old. Killing just don't give me a thrill any more. At my age I guess a man appreciates every day of life he has left, and he's not so anxious to take it away from anybody else. Even a damned chicken."

Ben leveled a finger at him. "But that's just me, lad. Marlow and Schafer don't feel that way about it. I don't have the heart to kill the wild man, but they do, and I won't pass judgment on them. And you shouldn't either. You're out here on a lark, but they're trying to scratch out a living. So am I. I'd like to have a good season and quit this hard life. I've got a few years left and I'd like to take it easy. You've got about four weeks left, and then something will have to be done."

Gil chewed the tough venison and remembered those last words. He had tried everything. Day after day he had gone down to the river and cut for sign and followed the barefoot tracks, and every time the trail had come to a dead end, either on rocky ground or in a stream of water. The tracks went in but they never seemed to come out again. They just vanished. The wild man knew he was being pursued, and unlike a coyote or a wolf or any other beast, he knew how to lose his trail. He seemed to have the cunning of an animal along with the intelligence of a man.

Gil had built snares, had stayed up long into the night designing them and drawing them out on paper. Often he would find his snares, not just empty, but sprung and destroyed, almost as though the wild man had set out to mock him. Gil had even tried to set a snare beside a snare, hoping the wild man would be drawn into destroying the decoy and step into the other while he was preoccupied. The wild man had destroyed them both.

Gil had considered running him down on horseback and roping him. That had been Esteban's idea, and Gil had thought it might work. Esteban had cowboyed in northern Mexico and could use a reata as though it were part of his arm. He had loaned Gil the treasured six-strand rawhide reata he had brought with him out of Mexico. It had been made by a master craftsman, and Esteban had kept it greased and supple for years, even though he used it very little now that he was running sheep. It was a full sixty feet long and had a hondo made of rolled rawhide.

Esteban had shown him how to use it, building a big fifteen-foot loop, holding two small coils in his roping hand, and throwing at targets thirty feet away. The extra coils in the throwing hand, Esteban had pointed out, allowed the loop to travel farther and with less resistance.

Gil had set up a bucket and practiced throwing the reata, hour after hour, until he could hit the target twenty-five times in a row without a miss. Then, confident that he could handle the reata, he had gone out hunting the wild man. He had prowled the Clear Fork country for days, cutting for sign, following tracks, until one day he finally got his chance.

It was a gloomy day around the first of November. He had been riding all morning, following those barefoot trails that vanished into the air. He broke through some brush on the banks of the Clear Fork and looked straight into the startled eyes of the wild man. He had been drinking at the river, and beside him were three white-tailed deer. They bolted and ran, and the wild man did the same. Gil spurred Snip and turned him into the chase. He built a big loop in the reata and dodged low limbs as they plunged through the brush.

The wild man was fast, faster than any human, and his endurance was beyond belief. In the brush along the river, he used all his speed and cunning to best advantage, and Gil couldn't get close enough to make a throw. Then they broke into a clearing. The wild man seemed to know that he had made an error. Looking back over his shoulder, he made a dash for the brush on the other side. Gil spurred Snip into a gallop, moved in, swung the reata, and made a long throw. It went straight to the mark and pulled tight around the wild man's waist.

Gil had rehearsed this moment in his mind many times, and he knew exactly what to do. He would dally the reata to his saddle horn, turn the horse, and drag the wild man until he was too weak and battered to put up a struggle, or drag him all the way back to Phantom Hill, if that was necessary.

Just as he was reaching for the saddle horn, the wild man stopped fighting the rope and came toward the horse, running, screaming, and waving his arms. Gil was caught off guard. Snip was terror-stricken. His ears shot up, his neck went out, and his eyes grew as round as plates. That was all he needed to see of the wild man. He wheeled around and headed for Phantom Hill, bucking every third step. Gil held onto the reata as long as he could and managed to jerk the wild man off his feet. But when Snip started splitting the timber and brush, he threw the rope away and tried to stay on the horse without getting his brains bashed against a tree limb.

They hit the river at a dead gallop. Snip had always been a bit shy about crossing water, but this time he didn't even slow down. The water was shallow about halfway across, but there the channel had dug out a hole three feet deep. Snip hit it full speed, lost his front feet, nosed into the water, and did a hoolihan. Gil was thrown clear and landed on his back near the north bank. Snip wallowed out of the hole and came out running, holding his head out to the side to keep from stepping on the reins. Gil walked back to Phantom Hill.

Later he went back to the clearing and found Esteban's reata. It had been chewed into four peices. Gil had to pay Esteban twenty dollars for it.

He had tried everything. He didn't know what else to do. There appeared to be no way of catching the wild man. He was too strong, too fast, and too smart—too smart for his own good. If he couldn't be captured, he would be shot.

Gil reached into his shirt pocket and brought out the letter from Martha Wynn. It was dated October 1, and it had reached him yesterday.

Dear Gil,

This morning I looked out the west window and thought of you. I wonder what you are doing today. From where I am sitting right now, I can see the glider swing in the garden. It brings back many memories, both pleasant and painful.

Yesterday Mother and I finally got all the wedding material packed away in boxes. We made little bags of cheesecloth and filled them with cedar chips and placed several in each box. Cedar repels moths, you know. Then Daddy carried the boxes up into the attic.

It was a sad occasion for Mother. Several times I saw tears in her eyes. She has had a hard time accepting all this. I am her only daughter, you know. I have brothers and one day they will marry, but it's not the same with boys. I suppose Mother thinks I am doomed to become an old maid.

I told her that things have turned out for the best. I realize now that I almost married a man I hardly knew. Maybe you reached the same conclusion about me.

How can young couples walk so blindly into something as solemn as marriage? It happens every day. I see it happening to my friends. Our fathers would never go into a business venture poorly informed or ignorant of the risks, yet these same men think nothing of leading their daughters down to the front of the church and giving them away to virtual strangers.

Sometimes I feel bitter about this. When it comes to love, marriage, and family, everything is left to chance.

I am glad you left, Gil. It was the right thing and I am happy for you. I only wish that I could go somewhere—England, I think, or maybe Italy. Someplace with poetry in the air. Maybe I would be disappointed, but as you realized, one needs to go and see for one's self.

But it will never happen for me. A woman doesn't travel alone, lest she be accused of being "loose," as we say in Weatherford. Sometimes I think I would like to become "loose." As far as I can tell, the major disadvantage is that all the women who are not loose agree that it is wrong. We never hear from the other side, so maybe there are things we don't know.

Later. I should not have said those things. Reading over the last paragraph, I blushed. I ought to tear this letter up and start all over, but if I did, I might never find the time to write another. I shall send it if you will promise to burn it immediately.

Do you remember James Kennington? He is reading law under Judge Barfield. He has been coming over to see me in the evenings. Mother thinks highly of him and Daddy says he will amount to something, if he will stop racing horses.

I hope this letter finds you in good health and spirits. Please write and tell me of your adventures on the frontier. If I cannot have my own adventures, I would like to share yours. I think of you often, Gil, but as the weeks pass, I find it harder to remember your face.

MARTHA WYNN

Gil folded the letter and placed it in his shirt pocket. He would not burn it. He lay back against the tree and closed his eyes. His mind formed an image of James Kennington, a tall, lean man with a high forehead and a small mouth. He must be close to thirty now, and the last time Gil had seen him, he had noticed that James was getting bald. James was a quiet fellow, the sort who stood in corners and watched what others were doing. By the time he decided to take a course of action, he had thought it through from start to finish.

He sat up. It suddenly occurred to him what Martha had told him in the letter. She had disguised the message but it was there, between the lines. He pulled it out and read it over again. "I think of you often, Gil, but as the weeks pass, I find it harder to remember your face." How could he have missed it before? What Martha had said was, "Gil, I don't want to marry James Kennington, but I probably will unless you come back."

He caught his horse, untied the hobbles, and started back to Phantom Hill. To hell with the frontier and the wild man. He had seen enough of sand fleas and chicken droppings and scarlet women. He wanted to go home.

He loped the last quarter mile to the settlement. He was excited about the trip. In just three days, he would be in Weatherford with Martha, and James Kennington would have to find someplace else to spend his evenings.

When he rode up to the stone house, he saw Ben sitting outside, looking off into the distance. A horse was tied to the hitching rack on the west side. Gil didn't recognize the dun, which was in poor flesh and appeared to have been ridden hard.

He stepped down from the saddle and slacked his cinch. He walked over to Ben. "I've just decided . . . Whose horse is that?"

Ben was chewing tobacco and had to clear his mouth before he could speak. He leaned over and spat. "Belongs to a woman. She rode a long ways to see you. She's inside."

Gil's jaw dropped. *"Martha's here?"*

Ben stared at him. "Who's Martha?"

"Who's the woman?"

Ben sniffed. "Victoria LaRouge."

11

The moment he saw Vicki, he knew that something was wrong. Her face was gaunt, her dark eyes haunted, her hair matted and tangled. She had a purple bruise on her left cheek.

She greeted him with a smirking, defiant air. "Sorry to bust in on you this way. I know I look bad."

She hardly looked like the same woman he had seen only a month before. She was wearing her red saloon dress, but it was torn in several places and covered with a fine layer of trail dust. She must have left Fort Griffin in a hurry.

She turned away from him. "For God's sake, stop staring and say something."

He walked over to her and put his hand on her shoulder. "Vicki, what . . ."

She pushed it away. "I didn't come here for your sympathy, so don't bother."

He dropped his hat on the floor and sat down on Ben's pallet. The room was almost dark, and she sat huddled in a corner. He could see the whites of her eyes and part of her face. She reminded him of an animal glaring out of its den. "All right, you didn't come for sympathy. What did you come for?"

"I want to make a deal with you, strictly business. I need money."

"What's the deal?"

"Have you caught your wild man?"

"No. I've decided to give it up. It was a crazy idea."

"I know how to catch him." There was a long silence. "How much is it worth to you? Four hundred dollars?"

"No, I'm afraid not."

"Three hundred?"

"No."

"Two?" He shook his head. "You liar!" She shrieked. "You told me you had money! You told me you wanted the wild man! You've wasted my time, damn you! I thought I could count on you. What a stupid wretch I am."

"What's wrong with you?"

"I rode for two days to get here. I came to deliver the wild man to you and now you don't want him. That's what's the matter with me. You've made me look like a dunce."

"Why did you leave Griffin?"

"Because I wanted to."

"How did you get the bruise on your face?"

"I got punched around."

"By Trumbull?"

She lifted her chin. "Do you want the wild man or not?"

He wasn't sure what to say. "Maybe. We can talk about it."

"How much would you pay?"

"Two hundred."

"I need more. It's worth more. I'll deliver him to you without a scratch on him."

"It can't be done."

"No? I'll do it. I'll have him standing in this room in two weeks. I want three hundred dollars."

"I'm sorry."

She screamed at him and called him more names. He

stood his ground, and after a while she slumped back against the wall, passed her hand over her forehead, and dropped her voice to a whisper. "All right, anything you say. I've got to have money. Please go away and let me sleep."

At first he thought of pointing out that this was *his* house, and that if she wanted to sleep, maybe she could go someplace else. But he didn't. She looked so bad, he decided that she needed the house more than he and Ben did. He walked outside and closed the door.

Ben was still sitting in the chair, stroking the back of the chicken's neck. "Well, what was all that about?"

"I'm not sure, but I think we've lost the house for the night."

Ben's eyes came up. "Maybe *you've* lost the house, lad, but not me. I've camped with her kind before and I know that her reputation ain't at stake. I'm going in, and if she don't like it, she can light a shuck."

Gil stepped back and let him pass. He went inside and said something to Vicki. She shrieked at him and told him to get out. He yelled back at her. There was a clink of something metallic, and Ben came out the door in a fast trot, wiping brown liquid from his face and clothes.

"What happened?"

"The wench got me with the spittoon." He grabbed the chicken and used her feathers as a rag. Gil was laughing. "Go ahead and laugh, and when you get done, you can find us a place to sleep, seeing as how she's your guest. I'm going to the river to wash up."

He pitched the chicken into the air and stormed down to the river. They spent a fairly comfortable night in the back of Marlow and Schafer's wagon, sharing the space with a big Newfoundland dog.

Early the next morning, Gil crept out of the wagon and

left Ben snoring under the canvas tarp. He pulled on his boots, shivering in the crisp morning air, and walked to the house. He paced back and forth in front of the door, trying to decide whether to wake Vicki or not. At last he went to the door and knocked. There was no answer, so he pushed it open and peeked inside. He saw her lying on his pallet, facedown, with her left arm thrown up over her head.

"Vicki?" She didn't respond, so he went in. Standing over her, he called her name again, and when she didn't respond this time, he bent down and shook her. He could hear her breathing, but he couldn't wake her up. He gave her a hard shake and spoke her name in a loud voice. She groaned, rolled over, and opened her eyes.

It took her a minute to wake up and remember where she was. She moaned, sat up, pulled the hair out of her eyes. When she did, Gil saw that her face was an unhealthy color and she had dark rings under her eyes. She stared at him for a long time.

"I need a cup of coffee and a bath. Would it be asking too much for you to boil me some coffee?"

He built a fire in the fireplace and put coffee on to boil. She brought a hairbrush out of her carpetbag and started brushing the tangles out of her hair. But it was hopeless, and she finally gave up. When the coffee was ready, he poured her some in a tin cup and gave it to her. She thanked him and held it with both hands. They were shaking.

He sat down across the room from her and sipped on a cup of coffee. "Tell me what happened."

"I got beat up," she said in a dead voice. "I had to leave. I can't take it anymore. I need money."

"What happened to the fifty dollars I gave you?"

She gave him a puzzled stare, as though she didn't know what he was talking about. "Oh, that. Well, it's all gone. He found it."

"He?"

"Trumbull. You wouldn't understand. I don't understand it either. We fight, he beats me, he's a horrible man. But when he really wants me, he gets me, every time. I go to him and I can't help it. But this time"—she shook her head —"I'm leaving for good. No more." She sighed and rubbed her eyes. "I've got to move far away. I told him I was finished. He said he would kill me. I think he will. I need money, but not a gift this time. I'll earn it. I'll catch the wild man for you."

He gazed at her a long time. The wildness was gone from her eyes and now she looked tired, very tired. "How could you catch him? I've been trying for months. He's too smart."

"Being smart won't help him. If he's a man, if he's *really* a man, I'll get him. That's my business."

It took a minute for her meaning to soak in. "Vicki, I don't think you understand. He's like an animal. He's a genuine *wild* man."

She smirked at him. "Honey, I got news for you. When it comes to this side of life, you're all wild men. This one can't be any worse than Trumbull."

"I can't let you do it."

"Why?"

"It's too risky."

Her eyes came up and stabbed him. "If you're trying to be noble, don't bother, all right? It's my life and I'll decide what to do with it. It's not up to you to allow me to do anything. I'm not interested in your opinions. What about the money?"

"I'll give you the money for nothing, as a loan."

Her eyes flamed. *"I don't want you to give me the money!* You've already given me money and I let Trumbull take it away from me. Maybe if I earn it the hard way, I'll hang on to it."

He was silent for a minute. "Do you think it would work?"

"Sure." Her eyes mellowed, and one corner of her mouth turned up in a smile. "I've only been turned down once in my life—by you. And I'd be willing to bet that if I was all fixed up and looking good, you couldn't turn me down again. You've never seen me at my best. If I ever decide I want you, I'll get you. I'd bet on it."

He smiled.

"Well"—she finished the coffee—"you think about it for a while. I'm going to the river to bathe. You want to come along? We can talk." She saw the hesitation in his face. "Don't worry, I'm not modest. Come on."

They found her a bar of lye soap, a soapweed root, and a couple of blankets, and walked down to the river. The sun was up now and burning some of the chill from the air, but it was still rather cool for bathing. Gil lay on the dry sand north of the river and watched her undress.

When she tiptoed toward the water, he watched her. He stared at the graceful curve of her back, her tiny waist, the soft roundness of her hips, the smooth white legs. She put one foot into the water and gave a little squeal, then waded in until the water came almost to her knees. She dipped the soap into the water and rubbed it over her body and scrubbed herself with the soapweed root.

Half an hour ago, he would have bet his entire fortune that Vicki couldn't seduce him, because he didn't want her, because she was repulsive to him. Now all his resolves were in shambles. He was no longer aware of her dirty hair or the dark rings under her eyes or the bruise on her cheek. He no longer cared about the person inside the body, the woman who had been pawed and slobbered on by the vilest of men.

It didn't matter that she disliked men, teased them, taunted them, debased them, took their money, and laughed at them when they had gone. Nothing mattered now but the soft white flesh that gleamed in the morning sunlight. To touch it and hold it, a man would do almost anything.

She bent over and dipped her hair into the water and began scrubbing it with the soapweed root. She was looking at him now, her black eyes gleaming through her hair, her mouth drawn into a lopsided smile. He ran his eyes over the arc of her back. His heart beat like a hammer in his ears. He couldn't stand it any longer. He jumped to his feet and left. He walked a hundred yards or more. He stopped and looked back. He wanted her so desperately that his body ached.

"If I ever decide I want you," she had said, "I'll get you." She wouldn't get him this time, but he would never make the mistake again of thinking that he was beyond the power of a woman. Vicki had destroyed that illusion rather handily.

He sat down beneath a tree and waited for her to come up the trail. She came, wearing a blanket over her shoulders and carrying her clothes. He got up and fell in step beside her.

She tossed him a sultry glance. There was anger in it but also a kind of grudging respect. "You're pretty tough, aren't you?"

"No, I'm not tough at all. You just proved it."

She gave her hair a toss and let it fall over her shoulder. "Why did you resist me?"

"Because I would have regretted it later."

"Who cares about later?"

"I do."

She laughed. It was a jagged laugh. "Next time you won't. I'll get you inside a house where you can't run away.

I'll show you things you've never dreamed of. I'll drive you out of your mind. You won't turn me down a third time, Gil Moreland. There's no man on earth who can do that."

He believed her.

"Well," she said, "do you think I can catch a wild man?"

"If a man wasn't wild before he saw you like that, he'd be wild after he did."

"Do we have a deal?"

"Vicki, I think it's wrong. I'm not sure why, but it just seems wrong. I wish you'd reconsider."

"I've done my considering. How much is it worth to you?"

"I'd pay two hundred, no more."

"It's a deal." She stopped. They were still several hundred yards south of the settlement, below a hill. She reached into her bag and brought out a bottle filled with amber liquid. She poured some into her hands and rubbed it all over her body. It had a heavy odor, something between perfume and medicine.

"What is that?"

"Myrrh. We've been using it since the beginning of time, so it must be good. I think your wild man will like it." She reached up with a finger and rubbed some myrrh on his cheek. "I only use it on special occasions. I'll save some for you."

She laughed and they walked back to the settlement. They stopped at the door of the house. "You want to come in for a while?" She mocked him with her eyes.

"No thanks. When do you want to start?"

"As soon as I get dressed." She gave him a list of things she would need, and he said he would get them.

"There's one thing I don't understand," he said. "I think he'll find you. I know you can lure him in. But how will you hold him?"

Her eyes were half-concealed by drooping lids. "Without chains or ropes or guns."

"But how?"

"That's my business. In two weeks he'll walk in this door and he'll be yours."

"But I don't see . . ."

He didn't finish the sentence. She had already gone inside and shut the door. He walked to the trader's store. His knees were still shaky and he had the scent of myrrh in his nostrils.

12

Gil chose a spot three miles up Clear Fork for Vicki's camp. He had found the wild man's tracks in this vicinity many times, and had surmised that there must be some kind of plant or tree growing nearby that provided him with food.

Ben came along to help build a dugout shelter. He wanted his bed back, and he must have figured that the quickest way of accomplishing that was to get Vicki moved out. Otherwise, he probably would have stayed home. He wasn't one to go looking for things to do, especially if they involved hard labor. And he didn't like Vicki.

There was a constant antagonism between the two of them. Ben said she put on too many airs for a woman of her profession, and she considered him a dirty, ill-mannered trapper, of a type she had seen too often at Fort Griffin. She called him "Beard" and he called her "Woman," and their conversations were carried on in snarls and profane language. For some reason, Vicki did not use vulgarisms around Gil, but with Ben around, she talked as crudely as any man on the frontier.

They chose a natural depression in the side of a hill, did some shovel work to dig it out, and started cutting and dragging logs for roof timbers. The dugout faced the river to the south and was well protected from the north wind. It was only about fifty feet from the front door to a pool of sweet spring water, and an abundance of firewood lay close at hand, mostly dead cottonwood trees that had washed down the river during the spring rises. They built a simple fireplace of rock at the back of the dugout, and left a vent hole in the dirt roof so the smoke could exit. If it came a hard rain, the vent would leak water, but they didn't want to take the time to build a chimney in such temporary quarters.

They didn't finish the work by the time the sun went down, so Vicki slept inside the dugout and the men camped a short distance away. The next morning they moved in all the supplies and food: dried beans, bacon, a big sugar-cured ham, coffee, sugar, flour, and salt. As he was transferring these items to the dugout, Gil found a large jar filled with a reddish liquid. He didn't remember buying it, and since the jar was not labeled, he asked Vicki about it. She snatched it out of his hands and carried it into the dugout herself. She didn't tell him what it was, and he didn't feel free to ask again. He figured it must be perfume or body oil.

The last chore was to cut and stack two weeks' supply of firewood, and when that was done, Ben went out to catch and saddle the horses and prepare for the trip back to Phantom Hill. Vicki had grown more irritable by the hour and made no attempt to disguise the fact that she was ready to get the men out of her camp.

"Well, I guess you're on your own from here," said Gil. "I don't feel quite right about leaving you out here."

"I can take care of myself."

He pulled his pistol and handed it to her. "I think you'd better keep this."

She gave him a look of complete scorn, hoisted her dress, and pointed to a two-shot derringer fastened to the back of her thigh with two strips of leather. "How dumb do you think I am? Why don't you just run along and let me get to work?"

"Sorry. Now Vicki, I want to warn you that the wild man has yellow eyes, wolf eyes, you might say. The first time you see them . . ."

"Will you get out of here and leave me in peace?" She shoved him toward the door.

"Do you want me to come back in a day or two?"

"No. It's either sink or swim for me. You just make sure you have your money ready."

"All right." He paused at the door and looked back at her. He thought he saw fear in her eyes. "If anything happens, you've got a horse. Ride for help."

"Leave."

"He's tied to a picket rope down on the meadow. You'll need to move him and take him to water once a day."

A sack of dried apples hit him on the side of the head and knocked off his hat. "Good-bye, Vicki." She didn't return the farewell.

Ben and Gil started back to Phantom Hill. Gil looked back over his shoulder for the first quarter mile, half expecting Vicki to come out and call them back. She didn't, and they rode over a hill and the dugout passed out of view.

"Quit worrying about her," Ben grumped. "She ain't worth it."

"Maybe not, but I can't help admiring her. She's got guts."

"Guts? No, I don't think so, lad. She's doing what she likes best, that's all." Ben had a big quid of tobacco in his mouth, and he shifted it over to the other cheek. "Dragging a man down to her level. Whipping him up into a frenzy and making him crawl to her feet and beg. A man gets his minute of pleasure with her, but he pays for it. While he begs and crawls, she watches him with those pretty black eyes and grins."

Gil almost said something in Vicki's defense, but caught himself. Why should he defend her? He had caught glimpses of that side. That's why he had resisted her. "How do you know so much about Vicki?"

Ben looked away. "Oh, you might say I was sweet on her for a while when she first hit this country. I'm a slow learner, but once I learn, I don't forget. She's mean and evil, and not just because she's a whore. I've met several who weren't that way at all. They'd give a man his pleasure and make him feel at home. Not her. She's got a grudge. She likes to throw a fishhook into you and give it a twist." He leaned away and sent a brown comet of tobacco juice arcing over his shoulder. "You know where she got that bruise on her face, don't you?"

"Trumbull."

"That's right. They deserve each other. She's just as rotten as he is. So if you want to worry about somebody, worry about the wild man. That poor devil never did anything wrong, but he's fixing to get an education about the human race."

"You don't exactly approve of all this, I suppose."

"What do I care? It ain't my problem. When you see a cat after a mouse, you'd just as soon not take sides, but now and then you get to wondering how it would feel to be the mouse."

"The wild man's not a mouse, Ben. I've got some scars to prove it."

"*You* went after *him,* lad, and he fought to protect himself. Any animal would. But he's got no protection against that woman." They rode up a steep bank, and up on top they could see the smoke rising from cooking fires at Phantom Hill. "But at least we won't have to shoot him. I'm kind of glad about that."

That afternoon, Ben went to work on his trapping gear. He had bought a dozen No. 4 Newhouse traps from the local trader and he fitted them all with steel stakes. They had been covered with a thin layer of oil at the factory, to keep them from rusting, and he wiped them off with a dry rag. Then he threw them into some weeds behind the house. Ben explained that animals could smell the oil and wouldn't go near a trap that was fresh out of a store. A good functional trap was one that had been left out in the weather to rust, until the smell of man had left it. Once the traps were seasoned, they had to be handled with care, lest they pick up the scent of skin oil, sweat, or tobacco.

Gil watched and listened, but his mind was somewhere else. He paced and fidgeted, whittled on a stick, and even tried some of Ben's horrid chewing tobacco. Around three o'clock he saddled Snip, borrowed Ben's pocket telescope, and rode up the Clear Fork. He studied the terrain carefully, since he didn't want to blunder into Vicki's camp by mistake. He staked out his horse a quarter mile downriver from the dugout and went the rest of the way on foot. He carried blankets and some dried food with him. He also carried his Henry rifle.

He had picked out a spot that morning when he and Ben had ridden back to the settlement, and he had memorized the landmarks around it. It was a high knob about seventy-five yards northwest of the dugout. It offered an unobstructed view of the river bottom and had enough brush and grass on top to conceal a man. He crept up the hill and crawled into the brush until he was sure that he couldn't be seen. With his knife he carved off branches, making himself a hollow place in the center, and laid the branches on the ground for bedding. He dragged his blankets over the branches and made a fairly comfortable bed. As long as it didn't rain or snow, he would be all right.

He parted the branches on the east and looked down. A ribbon of gray smoke rose straight up from the dugout. There was not a breath of wind, not a sound of any kind. After a while he saw Vicki come out of the dugout. She spread a blanket on the ground, sat down, and brought something out of her carpetbag. It was about fifteen inches long and appeared to be a stick of wood. She placed one end of it in her mouth and began to play it. Gil opened the telescope and saw that the object was a recorder, an ancient form of flute.

It was a haunting melody she played, perhaps more of Chopin's melancholy music. Like the wisp of smoke, it seemed to rise in the silent air, coiling around itself. Such lovely music drifting out over the meadow gave Gil an eerie feeling. She played with the same precision she had shown at the keyboard, and the song was beautiful beyond description. He laid aside the telescope and listened and watched, absorbed in the music.

He lost track of time. Maybe thirty minutes had passed, maybe an hour, when he saw something move on the periphery of his vision. He shifted his eyes to the spot and saw nothing, but he kept his eyes on it. After a bit he saw movement again and detected a slight change in the coloration of a patch of brush. He lifted the telescope to his eye and saw a human face peering through the branches. The hair was long, black, and tangled. The eyes were yellow.

He held his breath. The wild man was looking toward the dugout. Minutes passed. He stood as rigid as a tree, staring without blinking. Then he stepped out of the brush and into the clearing, about thirty yards in front of the dugout. Gil could see him glancing in all directions, as wary as a deer.

He lifted his nose and tested the wind. Did he smell the myrrh?

When Vicki saw him, the music stopped. They stared at each other, neither moving a hair. Then she began playing again, and he moved toward her, one cautious step at a time. With each step he stopped, glanced around, listened, and tested the wind. He moved closer and closer, until he was only ten feet away from her. There was a slight tremor in the music now, but Vicki continued playing.

Regardless of what Ben had said about her, no matter how wicked she was, Gil admired her. It took nerves of iron for her to sit there playing Chopin while that huge, yellow-eyed man crept toward her. She had guts.

The wild man cocked his head and listened to the music. Maybe this was the first music he had ever heard. He sank into a crouch, then went down to his hands and knees. He crept toward her. He was on the edge of the blanket now, only two feet away from her. He reached out his hand and ran it through her hair.

The music stopped. Through the scope, Gil saw that Vicki was sitting as rigid as a cocked spring, her face taut with lines of fear. The wild man stroked her hair for a long time, then ran his hand down her arm and looked at her hands as though he had never seen hands before. With his index finger he traced the lines of her mouth and nose. He took the flute from her, stared at it, and put it to his mouth. When he blew on it, the instrument gave out a high-pitched squeal. He leaped to his feet and ran a short distance away. Vicki picked it up and started playing. He stopped and moved toward her again.

Gil could see a change come over her face. She seemed more at ease now, and she was smiling. She laid down the flute, slipped out of her blouse, and tossed it out on the ground in front of the wild man. She wore nothing beneath it. The wild man stared at her and picked up the blouse and smelled it.

Vicki stood up and he took a step backward. She unbuttoned her skirt and let it fall around her ankles. The wild man's lips moved and his yellow eyes began to blaze. She kicked the skirt out in front of him and sat down on the blanket. She pulled a second blanket around her shoulders and reached for something behind her back. Gil turned the scope on it and saw a big jar and a tin cup. It was the same jar he had seen that morning. She poured some of the liquid into the cup.

It must be whiskey, Gil thought, though he had never seen any whiskey that dark and red.

The wild man picked up the skirt and smelled it and rubbed it over his face. Gil turned the scope on Vicki. She was talking to him now. Gil couldn't hear any of the words because she spoke in a low voice. The muscles in the wild man's jaws rose and fell. He ran his tongue over his lips. He held her clothes against his chest and walked toward her. He knelt beside her on the blanket. She ran her finger around his face, down his neck, down his arm, back up to his neck, and through the thick hair on his chest. While she did this, he sat rigid, staring into her eyes.

She handed him the cup and told him, through signs, to drink. He held it and looked into it, then put it to his lips and drank.

Darkness was falling over the Clear Fork meadows when Vicki rose to her feet and walked into the dugout. A moment later, the flute music drifted out into the air. With the grace of an acrobat, the wild man pushed himself off the blanket, glanced around, and went inside.

Gil rolled over on his back and chewed up some jerky and dried fruit. He could see the stars through the brush overhead. That was a good sign: no rain. He wanted to stay through the night to make sure nothing happened to Vicki. It was six-thirty and already dark, and he had nothing to do but lie there and think.

His thoughts drifted back to Weatherford and Martha Wynn. Just three days ago, he had read her letter with its message about James Kennington, and he had gone back to Phantom Hill with the intention of leaving the frontier and returning to Weatherford. But Vicki had been waiting for him, and everything had changed. So much had happened in three days since, it seemed weeks ago.

He had intended to write Martha a long letter, but he just hadn't found the time for it. Now he had the time but no light, no paper or pen. He knew he should write her soon. He wanted her to know that he was thinking about her and that he was looking forward to seeing her again.

He wished he could tell Martha about Vicki and the wild man, and describe to her the scene he had just witnessed. It didn't seem right, somehow, and it troubled him.

He closed his eyes just for a moment, and when he opened them again, he saw the sky streaked with reds and pinks. He sat up and rubbed his eyes. The air was damp and cool, and diamonds of dew sparkled on the tall grass in the Clear Fork meadow. It was morning.

He rolled over and looked down toward the dugout. A thin line of smoke rose from the vent and three young deer grazed in the meadow. Gil's belly growled with hunger and he chewed up the last strip of jerky. All at once the wild man appeared at the door. Gil opened the telescope and peered into it.

He was wearing a serape over his shoulders. Vicki must have made it for him, cutting a hole in the middle of a wool blanket. And there was something different about his hair. It had been gathered at the back of his head and tied with a piece of string. Gil was surprised at how these small changes had altered his appearance.

The wild man reached his arms toward the sky, threw back his head, and yawned and stretched. He saw the deer and started walking toward them. They had been watching him from the moment he had walked out the door. They froze, with stalks of grass hanging from their mouths. He had gone ten or twelve steps toward them when their white tails shot up and they bounded off toward the river. He stopped and stared at them. He lifted one arm. When they disappeared into the timber, the arm fell to his side.

The wild man stood there for several minutes. A squirrel scurried down an oak tree and stopped not far from him. He walked toward the squirrel. The creature went up on his hind legs, flicked his bushy tail, and chattered, ran to the tree with long bounds, and climbed to the top branches. The wild man stopped and gazed up to the top of the tree. He held his hands up in front of his face and looked at them, then turned them over and looked at the back side. He walked to the spring pool and knelt down and brought his face close to the surface. Gil thought he was going to drink, but he didn't. He looked at his reflection in the water.

Just then, Vicki appeared at the door. She wore a blanket over her shoulders, and Gil could see her bare legs beneath it. She called to the wild man. He straightened up and looked at her over his shoulder. He got to his feet, removed the serape and threw it on the ground, tore the string out of his hair, and headed for the river in a long, loping stride.

Vicki went back into the dugout, and before long the wind brought the smells of food cooking. Around ten o'clock she came out again, spread her blanket on the ground, and read some of the newspapers she had brought with her, old copies of the Dallas *Herald* and the Denison *News* she had found at the trader's store. She seemed perfectly content with herself, as though she were spending the day at a Galveston beach.

Gil waited and watched. The hours dragged by and nothing happened. Then, in the early afternoon, the wild man returned. He walked slowly, with his head down. Vicki must have heard him, for she watched his approach over the top of her paper. He walked right up to her and stood. She handed him a piece of ham that she had been nibbling on. He took a taste of it and threw it down. She poured him a cup of the red liquid, and when she offered it to him, he slapped it out of her hand. He left and Vicki went back to her reading.

During the afternoon he returned two more times. Each time he stood over her and refused everything she offered him and left shortly thereafter. At dusk Vicki moved her things inside. The wild man had not come back.

By this time Gil's muscles ached from lack of exercise. He was hungry and tired of lying in one position for so long, but he couldn't bring himself to leave.

Darkness came and he drifted off to sleep. He awoke sometime in the night. He didn't know the hour or what had awakened him. Then he heard the sound, and he knew what had awakened him.

It came from somewhere down in the dark Clear Fork bottom. It was a sound like nothing he had ever heard before, and it made the hair stand up on the back of his neck. It was a cry, human but not human, a cry of pain and rage, and it echoed through the valley. As the echo of one cry fell into silence, there came another right behind it. Several times he heard the crash and pop of limbs, as though the wild man were tearing them off of trees.

The crying went on throughout the night, and Gil did not sleep well. He lay huddled in his blanket, watching and waiting between fits of sleep.

In the first light of dawn, just as he was about to doze off, he heard another cry, this one quite near. He looked out and saw the wild man walk out of the river bottom. His arms hung at his sides and he weaved from side to side like a drunken man. He walked to the place where he had left the serape the day before and stood over it. He picked it up and pulled it over his head. He lurched toward the dugout, and as he did, the haunting notes of the flute floated out into the morning air.

Gil opened the telescope and put it on the wild man's face. The wild yellow gleam was gone from his eyes, and in its place was a look of desolation. The wild man paused at the door, glanced back toward the river, and plunged inside.

13

It was eight o'clock at night. A big, cheery fire blazed in the fireplace while outside a norther moaned in the trees. Ben sat in the chair, sewing up a hole in his long-john underwear. The chicken slept on his lap. The bird had been living in the house for more than three months now, and two days ago Ben had finally given her a name. By naming her, he had admitted the obvious, that the bird had moved in. He called her Chickie.

Gil thought the name was hilarious and he smiled every time he heard it. Ben Woolsey simply didn't seem the kind of man who would make a pet of a chicken, let alone give it such a ridiculous name.

Gil was finally getting around to writing his letter to Martha Wynn, and now that he had started it, there seemed no way of bringing it to an end. He had already written five pages in his careful script. He had told her about Ben and Chickie and Esteban Martinez's children. Now he was trying to describe the wild man. He would not tell her about Victoria LaRouge. Maybe at some later date he would, but not now. He didn't think she would approve. He *knew* she wouldn't approve.

"The trader got in three box-loads of long johns and flannel shirts," said Ben, squinting over his sewing. "And

Christmas is coming. Thought I might mention that, just in case somebody might be shopping around for me a present."

"If anybody asks, I'll sure tell them."

"Heh." Ben smiled. "When are you expecting The Red back?"

"She said two weeks, Ben. Tomorrow will be the end of the second week."

"I hope she goes straight back to Griffin and don't hang around here."

"I doubt that she'll go back to Fort Griffin at all. She had that trouble with Trumbull, you know, and she's afraid he'll try to kill her."

"Well, I hope she goes somewhere. I ain't giving up my bed in this weather."

Gil heard the door open and felt a rush of cold air moving across the floor. He thought it might have blown open. He looked up from his letter and stared straight into C. D. Trumbull's small black eyes. His face, above his heavy beard, was red from the cold, and his notched ear showed beneath his cap. In his gloved hand, he held a big Colt Walker pistol.

Gil froze and cut his eyes toward Ben. He had stopped his sewing and was looking at Trumbull. Gil could see the pulse rising and falling in the big vein on his neck. Ben's hand moved to the spot where he usually carried his pistol, but it wasn't there. Neither Ben nor Gil was wearing a pistol belt. They had been caught by surprise.

"Evening, boys. Mind if we come in and warm our bones?" Trumbull looked outside and yelled, "Come on, Junior, hurry up."

Junior came in and closed the door. He was a small, skinny man with sallow skin and eyes like two purple grapes. He had a long, pointed chin and no teeth, and a week's worth of gray whiskers bristled on his face. He was dressed in a greasy sheep-lined coat and wore a rag around his ears to protect them from the cold. He carried a double-barreled shotgun.

"Any sign of her horse?" Trumbull asked.

"Didn't see a thing, C. D."

Trumbull grunted his displeasure. He saw Gil's pistol belt lying at the foot of his bed and Ben's hanging from a peg on the wall. He removed the pistols and stuffed them into his belt.

"There, now you boys rest easy. We ain't hunting your hides tonight, so just ooze back and relax." Trumbull removed his fur cap, dropped it on the floor. "Where is she?"

"Who?" Ben asked.

"You know who. The Red. I was told she came here to see Pretty Boy." Trumbull gestured with his pistol toward Gil. "They're good friends, don't you see. Where's she at?"

"She ain't here. If she was, I imagine she'd be inside on a cold night like this."

"That's sorter what I figgered, Woolsey, and I'm awful disappointed that she ain't. I just knew we'd find her here by the fire, talking with Pretty Boy about . . . *mew-zick.*"

This brought a laugh from Junior. He had a squawky voice and his Adam's apple jumped up and down when he laughed.

Trumbull flicked his eyes over to Gil. "The Red thought that was pretty funny, said she'd never run into a man who was so fond of . . . *mew-zick.*" Junior laughed again. "Said y'all just talked and played and played and talked and had a big old time. You getting mad, Pretty Boy? Did you think The Red liked you because you was such a gentleman? Huh. Soon as you left town, she came straight to me, gave me that fifty dollars, and told me all about you. She thinks you're a big sap with lots of money."

"Yeah," Junior squawked, "but he likes *mew-zick.*"

Gil's face burned. How could Vicki have betrayed his trust to someone as low as C. D. Trumbull?

Trumbull went on. "Course you know what *she* is. She's a Judas. She'd sell you out to me, then turn right around and sell me out to you. She's got no sense of loyalty, not even as much as that chicken there. Don't waste your time trying to protect her. She ain't worth it. I guarantee she'd cut your throat for a silver dollar. Mine too."

He turned to Ben. "I don't want no trouble or bloodshed, Woolsey. We've had our differences, me and you, but I got other business tonight. Me and you come from the same breed of dogs. We understand each other. We can talk things over and be reasonable. I want The Red. You tell me where she's at and me and Junior'll just mosey along and let you boys enjoy your evening by the fire. What do you say?"

Ben stroked Chickie on the back of the head and watched Trumbull. "She ain't here."

"Hey, C. D." Junior bent over and pulled something out of a pile of clothes in the corner. It was a red scarf, a woman's scarf. Vicki must have left it. He held it up and Trumbull snatched it out of his hands. He smelled of it and his face hardened.

"All right, boys, start talking or we start shooting."

Ben was still stroking the chicken, and his expression had not changed. In the silence Gil heard the hammers click on Junior's shotgun.

All at once the door opened and in walked Esteban Martinez. "Benito, I need to borrow . . ." He saw the men and the guns. He stopped. His mouth dropped open and he raised his hands over his head.

Trumbull walked over to him and put the barrel of his pistol in Esteban's face. "Hi there, Meskin. How would you like to die?"

"No, please, I have children."

"No kidding?" Trumbull clamped his left hand on Esteban's neck and shook him. "Well, if you want to go home to Mama and the *muchachos,* tell me where I can find Vicki the Red. She came here maybe two weeks ago, wore a red dress, had dark eyes, good-looking woman."

"I saw her," Esteban gasped, "but she left. I do not know where she went, I swear it to God."

Esteban was telling the truth. He didn't know where the dugout was or exactly what Vicki had been doing at Phantom Hill. Trumbull's lip curled, showing his brown teeth, and he cocked the hammer on the Colt Walker.

"Hold it, Trumbull. I'll tell you what you want to know." Ben looked at Gil. "She ain't worth Steban, lad." He told Trumbull that Vicki was living in a dugout and gave him directions for getting there. The directions were accurate except that he said the dugout was five miles upriver instead of three.

Trumbull smiled and released his grip on Esteban's neck. "That's better. Meskin, go on home to Mama and keep your mouth shut. If you step outside your door tonight, you'll be a dead man."

"Yes, sir." Esteban gave Ben a glance and ran out the door.

Trumbull turned to Ben. "Now, you boys stay by the fire and keep warm and leave us to our business. If you follow us, somebody'll get hurt." He bent down and picked up his fur cap. "You know, Woolsey, cold weather bothers this right ear of mine. If I don't keep it covered, it torments me. Nice seeing you boys again. Let's go, Junior."

They backed out the door, Trumbull first. He was outside when Junior reached the door. "Kill 'em, Junior."

Smoke and flames leaped from the barrel of the shotgun, and the roar was deafening. Ben never had a chance. The buckshot hit him squarely in the chest and threw him over backward out of the chair. Through the smoke, Gil saw Junior's big grape eye sighting down the gun barrel as it swung around for the second shot. He knew he was going to die, and in that instant before the gun went off, he thought of Martha. She would never receive his letter. He felt the explosion of the gun and saw the fire coming toward him. He hit the floor and lay still.

"Got 'em, C. D. Blowed Woolsey clean across the room."

"There's two snakes dead and one more to go. Let's move on."

The hoofbeats faded into the distance. Gil opened his eyes and wondered if he were dead or alive. The room was filled with smoke and the smell of sulfur. Esteban came running in, carrying his old Springfield with the cracked stock. His eyes widened in horror. *"Ay dios,* Benito!" He crossed himself and bowed his head for a moment. Then he came over to Gil and asked how badly he was hurt.

He didn't know. He couldn't feel any pain and he hadn't found any blood. He sat up and, to his astonishment, found that he had not been touched. The buckshot had struck the wall in a tight pattern only inches above his head.

"I guess I'm all right, Esteban. But Ben . . ." He glanced over at his friend. Ben's glazed eyes stared into space. His right hand was still on the chicken, where it's head had been. Their blood ran together into a crimson pool on the floor. One of the chicken's legs was still kicking. Gil turned away and leaned his head against the cold stone wall.

He felt Esteban's hand on his shoulder. "I am sorry. Why did they do this? Who were they? I will saddle my horse and we will go after them."

Gil took a deep breath and tried to steady himself. All at once he was trembling all over. "No, you stay here, Esteban. It's not your fight. Your family needs you. If I'm not back by tomorrow noon, go ahead and bury Ben."

He knelt over the body and looked into Ben's face. "You were good to me, Ben Woolsey. I'm sorry. I'll miss you, old friend." He closed the glazed eyes and covered the body with a blanket. Two of Esteban's children had come in and they were crying.

Gil put on some warm clothes, filled all his pockets with ammunition, and said good-bye to Esteban.

The bitter north wind cut at his face as he rode down into the Clear Fork bottom, and he could feel his breath freezing in his mustache. But he hardly noticed the cold. His mind was still numb, and he felt as though he were riding through a dream. He was vaguely aware that Ben would no longer be around to steer him away from danger. "You're on your own now," he said to himself. "You're on your own."

He rode down the river until he came to the base of the hill where he had observed Vicki and the wild man two weeks ago. He left his horse and climbed to the top. When he parted the bushes and looked down toward the dugout, he saw that Trumbull had found it, in spite of Ben's directions. He caught a glimpse of two horses galloping into the timber. He jerked the Henry to his shoulder and levered in a bullet, but the riders had already vanished into the night.

The door hung open when he reached the dugout, and shadows from the fire danced out on the ground. He paused at the door, wishing he didn't have to go inside. He had seen enough carnage for one night and he wasn't sure he could stand any more. He filled his lungs with cold air, set his jaws together, and went in.

He heard Vicki moaning and saw her lying facedown on the floor. He glanced around. The wild man was gone. He set the Henry against the wall and bent down over Vicki. He turned her over and had to look away. Trumbull had given her a beating and had worked her over with a knife. She had lost a great deal of blood. Her skin was gray and cool, and he could hardly find a pulse.

He found a clean cloth and wiped some of the blood away from the cuts on her face. He called her name and she opened her eyes. "It's going to be all right, Vicki, don't worry. I'm here."

Her lips were cut and swollen, but she managed a weak smile. "Trumbull got me . . . said he would." He asked her where she hurt. She shook her head. "Don't know, can't feel." Her eyes were glassy, but after a bit they came into focus. "Tell you something. Come close, listen." He bent closer to her mouth. "Wild man heard them coming, went out, got away."

"Vicki, save your strength."

She shook her head. "Listen. Big jar, tin cup. Laudanum."

He stared into her eyes. "You gave *laudanum* to the wild man? Why?"

She closed her eyes, and for a moment he thought she had died. "Needed money."

He looked away. She had addicted him to laudanum. That had been her plan all along. That's why she had been so positive that she could capture him. Gil felt sick at his stomach.

Her lips moved and he bent down again. "He's got to have it. Half a cup each day, eighteen grains. Buy more Fort Griffin, Dr. Gibson." Her voice faded to a whisper and all at once there was a look of urgency in her eyes. "Closer, come closer." He put his ear down to her mouth. "He's human. He can talk. Don't let him suffer. I wish . . . I'm sorry . . . sorry . . . Daddy!"

Her eyes widened and a quiver passed through her body. She shuddered, gasped, and lay still. He saw the life disappear from her eyes. He rose to his feet and walked to the door. Outside, the wind moaned in the naked trees. He didn't even know her real name. Her family would never know that she had died on the Texas frontier.

It must have been past midnight, though he didn't know for sure. His sense of time had become disjointed. Ben was dead. Vicki was dead. The murderers had escaped. And somewhere out in the night roamed a man-animal who was addicted to tincture of opium. He wasn't able to comprehend it all. He wanted to go home and forget all the horrors of the night. But home was far away.

He must have dozed off on his feet. He awoke with a jolt, opened his eyes, and saw the wild man standing outside the door, not more than ten feet away. Gil's hand went for his pistol. It wasn't there, and he remembered that Trumbull had taken it.

He searched the wild man's face. The eyes were no less yellow than before, but somehow the wolfish quality had been muted. Instead, he saw anguish and fear and—was he just imagining this?—a kind of intelligent gleam. It was almost impossible to describe these subtle changes, yet they were there. He knew that the wild man had not come to fight.

He wore the blanket serape around his shoulders, and beneath it a pair of breeches. His feet were wrapped in pieces of blanket and tied with strips of leather. Vicki must have made the clothes out of the materials at hand. His hair was combed, parted down the middle, and plaited in a single braid that hung past his shoulders.

He opened his mouth and spoke in a voice that was surprisingly soft. "Vee-kee. Vee-kee."

The wild man had spoken a word. He had spoken Vicki's name.

"Vicki is dead. Bad men killed Vicki. Vicki dead." Using

pantomime, he tried to get the point across. The wild man watched him, but Gil got the feeling that he didn't understand. He stepped out the door and pointed inside. "Vicki is dead. Go see her."

Shadows from the fire played over the wild man's face. He went inside and Gil followed. He still wore a knife on his belt, and if the wild man went berserk and tried to kill him, he would use it.

Gil had spread a blanket over the body, and this seemed to puzzle the wild man. He looked back, as if to ask what he should do. With signs, Gil told him to pull back the blanket. He knelt down and pulled it back. Breath rushed into his lungs when he saw her bruised face and the lifeless stare of her eyes.

"Vee-kee, Vee-kee!" He touched the skin on her cheek and looked up at Gil. "Vee-kee?"

"Vicki is dead."

"Vee-kee det." He took her shoulders in his big hands and gave her a gentle shake. Gil saw a shudder pass through his body, and when he looked up again, his eyes were a yellow blur. They were filled with tears. "Vee-kee det! Vee-kee det!" He laid his head across her breast and wept like a child.

Minutes passed. The wild man's crying fell to a moan, then he was silent. He straightened up, looked down at Vicki's face one last time, and covered her with the blanket. He stood up. "Vee-kee det."

Gil nodded. "Yes, Vicki's dead, God rest her soul."

"Red wah-tur."

"What?"

"Red wah-tur."

"Red water?"

"Red wah-tur." The wild man pointed toward the big jar. He wanted the laudanum.

"No, I don't . . ."

"Red wah-tur."

Gil was so tired, he could hardly think straight anymore. He had to sleep, and he had no idea what the wild man would do if he were denied the laudanum. He poured the cup half full and handed it over. The wild man gulped it down. Within minutes his head began to slump and his eyelids drooped. He dropped the cup and lurched over to the south wall of the dugout. He sat down, drew his knees up, and rested his head on them. After a while, he toppled over and slept where he landed on the floor.

Gil wrapped himself in a blanket and lay down in front of the fire. He wondered if he would survive the night, but he was too tired to care.

Part Two

The Journey

14

It was April, and at last spring had come to the Clear Fork country. In just a matter of days the trees along the river had shot out their leaves and the grass had begun to grow. In the soft morning air, Gil could smell green grass and wild flowers.

He was standing in the doorway, gazing across the rolling prairie toward the horizon. The change of season had stirred something deep inside him. He felt restless and often caught himself gazing at the distant horizon. Phantom Hill was buzzing with activity now as the trail drivers pushed west with herds of cattle and parties of hunters moved out to the buffalo range. Each time Gil watched a group of horsemen leave the settlement, his eye followed them to the horizon and his heart went on with them, out West where a man and his dreams confronted each other.

His thoughts were broken when he saw Miguel Martinez, Esteban's oldest boy, coming toward him at a run. Something about the way the boy ran alarmed him, and he had a feeling that William was in trouble again. He heaved a sigh, went back into the house, pulled on his boots, and strapped on his pistol belt.

Miguel was at the door now, panting for breath. "Señor Geel, you better go to the saloon. William is fighting again."

"All right, Miguel. Thank you."

He slammed his hat down on his head and started toward the saloon. He was mad, but he wasn't sure at whom. He knew that William didn't try to cause trouble. He wasn't a fighter by nature and he didn't go out looking for trouble. But trouble followed him around and found him, whether he was looking for it or not.

Phantom Hill was getting a lot of transient people now that spring had come: hunters, trappers, traders, criminals on the run from the law, deserters from the military. On the whole, they were a sorry lot. They sat around Durkee's Saloon, drinking and trading yarns and bullying anyone who happened to strike them wrong.

Gil had cut William's hair to a conventional length and had dressed him in conventional clothes. At a distance he could easily pass for a normal man. He still moved in a kind of lumbering gait, and of course he was uncommonly large, but those were details that could be overlooked.

What could *not* be overlooked were his yellow eyes, and his habit of staring at people without blinking. In a crowd of rough men, that wolfish stare worked like a match tossed onto a pile of dry straw. It started trouble, even though Gil was convinced that William meant no harm by it. It was just his nature to stare at people. Had his eyes been blue or brown, he could have gotten by with it. But his eyes were not blue or brown. They were as yellow as the blazing sun.

Gil hurried past the ruins of the old barracks and headed straight for Durkee's Saloon, a crude picket building with a sod roof, a stone chimney, and a brush arbor porch along the front. He could hear men yelling and laughing. It was the laughter of men who wanted to see blood. Gil had heard it at cockfights and dogfights, and it never failed to provoke an instinctive revulsion in him. It was the sound of human males at their lowest level.

A crowd of men blocked the door. Most of them he had never seen before. They had gathered like vultures at the scene of a kill. He tapped the first man he came to on the shoulder.

"Excuse me, I need to get through."

The man turned and glared at him. "Stand in line like the rest of us."

Gil took him by the collar and the belt and threw him out of the way. He pushed two more men aside and bulled his way through the door. It was dark inside, and it took his eyes a while to adjust. William was fighting three men, all smaller than he. His nose was dripping blood and one of his eyes was swollen shut. He charged at the men, grabbed one, and threw him across the room like a doll. But the other two moved in and landed punches while he was occupied.

It was the same old story. William didn't know how to defend himself in a brawl, even though he had tremendous strength. A small man who knew how to jab and back away, keeping himself out of William's grasp, could pick him to pieces.

Gil pulled his pistol and fired two shots into the sod roof. The fight stopped. He walked across the floor and stood between the combatants. "All right, boys, that's enough. Go to the bar and have a beer on me."

Durkee, the owner, was leaning over the bar, his chin resting in the palms of his hands. It wasn't clear whether he wanted the fight to stop or continue. The men were wrecking the place, but Durkee was astute enough to know that a fight drew customers.

The largest of the three men came up to Gil. He had long, greasy hair and several teeth missing from the side of his mouth. He jerked his thumb toward William. "He belong to you?"

"You might say that."

"Take him back and put him in a cage. He don't belong here."

"What did he do to you?"

"He was bothering a woman, a friend of mine."

"Hold on, Calvin," called Durkee. "You better tell the whole story. They put him up to it, Moreland. They told your friend that Baltimore Sally wanted to talk to him. They sort of lured him in here and he went up to her. Must have scared her and she left. They was just funning, no harm done."

Gil felt his temper rising. "I see. Well, how was it, Calvin? Did you have a good time?"

Calvin grinned. "Yeah, it was fun. Your friend sure is dumb."

"They say he's an animal," said one of the others.

"A dumb animal," Calvin said. "He's got no business talking to our womenfolk."

"We'll all sleep a little easier tonight," said Gil, "knowing that you're protecting our womenfolk, Calvin. It's very noble of you. Come on, William, let's go." William's jaws were set and he glared at the men. He followed Gil across the floor.

"Get him out of here."

"Throw him a dead rabbit." The crowd laughed.

"Put him back in his cage!"

"Damned yellow-eyed animal!"

Gil ignored them and led William to the door. The entrance was blocked by dirty men with vapid stares. "Get out of the way, please."

He heard Calvin say something under his breath. He didn't catch all of it, but what he heard was, "Trumbull should have . . ." He stopped, turned on his heel, and stalked back.

"What did you say?"

"Nuthin'."

"You used the name Trumbull. Tell me what you said, and say it to my face."

Calvin threw back his head and curled his lip. "I didn't say nuthin', and you and your animal can just get the hell out of . . ."

Gil took him by the throat and threw him to the floor. The fight was on. One of Calvin's pals jumped Gil from behind, and the other came diving in on his head. The men who had been standing outside came pouring in. Some went after William and some went for Gil. William sent the first two or three flying across the room before he was dragged down. Gil knew they didn't have a chance against so many, so he landed two hard punches to Calvin's face before he was overwhelmed. Three men pinned Gil's arms while Calvin rolled up his shirt sleeves and wrapped his right hand in a rag.

"You're scum, Calvin," Gil said, "just common scum."

Calvin laughed and drew back his fist. "This is from Trumbull, old friend of mine." The blow landed hard on Gil's forehead, sending a shower of colored circles up behind his eyes. He hardly felt the rest of the blows. Several men took him by the feet and dragged him outside and threw him into a ditch. His head was reeling and he could feel blood pumping into his battered face. A moment later a crowd of men came out of the saloon. They were carrying William. They brought him up to the side of the ditch, swung him three times, and let him fly.

Laughing and yelling, they trooped back inside for a drink.

William lay facedown in the mud. His hands dug into the mud and clenched. He pounded his fists and uttered a cry of smothered rage. Gil crawled over and patted him on the shoulder.

"Let's go home and wash up. Come on, it's all right."

Gil helped him up and they staggered down to the river. They washed off the mud and the blood and Gil checked them both for missing teeth and broken noses. They had come through the beating in fair shape. Gil's ribs hurt on the right side, and William's face was swollen.

They walked back to the house and collapsed on their pallets. William had not uttered a word through the whole ordeal. But now that they were alone, he turned to Gil. His left eye was swollen to a narrow slit, and it was an angry shade of purple.

"Why? What I do?"

Gil lay back and closed his eyes. "I don't know why. People are cruel. They call *you* an animal, but they behave worse than animals. Welcome to the human race, that's all I can say."

William said nothing for a minute, then he asked the same question again. Talking with William on abstract matters, Gil could never be sure how much he absorbed and how much he didn't. Over the months they had spent together, Gil had studied him carefully and had begun to suspect that William had a sharp mind and that he understood virtually everything that was said to him. But for some reason he chose not to show it. He hid behind that immobile face and left you wondering.

Gil sighed. "Because you're different, William. It's that simple and that complicated. People look at you and sense that there's something odd about you. They're drawn to whatever that is, and they start picking at it. It's not your fault, and I don't know what to do about it. I can't change the world just for you. Do you understand any of this?"

He met the inscrutable stare, more gold than yellow now in the half-light of the house. "Red water."

"It's too early. I'll give it to you at bedtime, just as I always do."

"Red water."

There was an ugly burr in his voice. "No, William, you know the rules. We've discussed . . ."

"Red water now! Want red water now!" William's big hands were balled up into fists, and just for a second, Gil thought he would attack. He had never shown this much belligerence before, and it left Gil with an uneasy feeling.

"All right, I'll let you have the damned stuff, but we're not going to make a habit of this." He found the cup and the jar and poured in the eighteen-grain dose. William gulped it down and held out the cup for more. He had never asked for more. "Why do you want more? You know our rules. I can't do it."

"Want more."

"No."

"Want more!" He banged the cup on the hearthstones and gave Gil a threatening glare.

They stared at each other for a long time. "All right, I'll give it to you. If you want to become more dependent on this vile stuff and spend your life in a stupor, I guess I shouldn't care." He poured more laudanum into the cup and returned the jar to the cabinet. He secured the hasp and locked it.

William drank it down and threw the cup on the floor. "Pick up your cup. This isn't a pigpen."

William left the cup where it lay. He found Vicki's flute among his belongings and staggered over to the far corner of the room, as far away from Gil as he could get. The laudanum was already taking effect. Gil knew the signs very well by now. His shoulders and head began to slump, giving the impression that he was collapsing into his own body. He sat cross-legged on the floor and started playing "Yankee

Doodle Dandy." Gil taught him the song back in February. William had played it over and over and over.

Gil lay down and tried to sleep, but his mind kept throwing up images of William's snarling face as he had yelled, "Red water! Want more!" All at once, he realized that he was tired of William and wanted to get rid of him. He was sick of giving him opium day after day and watching him sink into that drugged stupor. He was sick of the fights, the constant trouble, the harassment, the looks that people gave him when he walked through the settlement. He was sick of Phantom Hill and its ignorant people, and he was sick of "Yankee Doodle Dandy." He wanted to go to Weatherford and see Martha Wynn. He had written her four times and she had not answered his letters.

The notes of the flute seemed to bore into his thoughts, until he realized that he wasn't hearing "Yankee Doodle Dandy" anymore. It was the song Vicki had played in front of the dugout five months ago. He sat up, just in time to see the flute fall from William's hands as he toppled over into a deep opium sleep.

Gil got up and hobbled outside, his whole body stiff and sore from the beating. He saddled Snip and rode north out of the settlement until he saw Esteban's sheep grazing on the side of a hill. He found Esteban and his brother sitting under a cottonwood tree, each braiding a rawhide bosal. He sat down beside them and told Esteban about the trouble in the saloon. Esteban was the best friend he had at Phantom Hill now that Ben was gone.

"I don't know what to do. William becomes more of a problem every day. He's a millstone around my neck. I trapped him, I brought him here, I civilized him, I'm responsible for him. But I don't want to be responsible for him anymore. I have other things to do with my life, and

William just doesn't fit in. Everywhere I go, he's going to cause trouble."

Esteban nodded and kept on braiding the rawhide. "It is no good here. People are afraid of him." He looked up and gave a shy smile. "My Celia is still afraid, though I tell her there is no reason. She locks the door every night."

"Should we leave?"

Esteban looked at his work and nodded his head.

Gil sighed. "That would solve your problem, but what about mine? What should I do with him?"

Esteban shrugged his thin shoulders. "I know about sheep, that is all."

Gil stayed with them for another hour, enjoying the solitude and the companionship of these herdsmen. At dusk, he stood up and gave Esteban his hand. *"Hasta luego, amigo."*

"Que te vayas bien."

He rode back to Phantom Hill. He had decided on a course of action. It would not be pleasant, but it had to be done.

15

"Incredible," said Dr. Gibson when Gil had told him the story about the wild man. He sat behind his desk in the Fort Griffin hospital, puffing on a thin cigar and inhaling the smoke. His eyes came up. "By any chance, did Vicki tell you anything about me?"

Gil hesitated. "Yes, she did."

"Tell me what she said. The truth, please."

"She said you provided her with laudanum in exchange for favors. She also said you were an addict."

Gibson was a small man with a sad face and weary eyes. He blew a smoke ring and watched it disintegrate as it moved toward the ceiling. "Let me tell you something about laudanum, Mr. Moreland. As you know, it's an anodyne, much more potent and effective than either calomel or colocynth. Also a good deal more dangerous. The liquid form, which you're familiar with, contains raw opium in a solution of alcohol. A normal hospital dose is one grain, about twenty-five drops.

"I practiced medicine in Galveston until eighteen seventy. My foot was run over by a carriage in the spring, crushed badly. It didn't heal properly and I suffered with it. I began taking laudanum, and within three months I was addicted. I lost my practice, my wife, everything. I came here because they needed a doctor, no questions asked. I was taking three hundred grains a day when I arrived and was moving toward dysfunction. I had to do something, and I began weaning myself from the drug. I took my last dose in the spring of seventy-one."

He stubbed out the cigar. "I know all about the horrors of addiction, Mr. Moreland, and my heart goes out to people with the problem. When Vicki walked into this office the first time, I knew she was an addict. I recognized the signs. I had seen them in the mirror, and one doesn't forget what one sees in his own mirror. I begged her to enter the hospital. I knew I could help her. 'Not now,' she would tell me, 'maybe next month.' So I supplied her with laudanum. It was a mistake. I never should have allowed it to get started, because once you start these things, you can't stop. Your initial compassion is exploited and becomes a source of more suffering."

"But she finally broke the habit on her own, didn't she?"

A hint of a smile formed on Gibson's mouth. "Did she tell you that? No, Vicki was addicted to laudanum when you met her and until the moment she died. She tried to get away from it, but she lacked the will. She knew exactly how to capture and enslave your wild man because she herself was enslaved.

"A large share of the blame must go to Trumbull. You know about him, of course. Fine fellow. About a year ago—yes, it was the spring of seventy-three—I told Vicki that my conscience wouldn't allow me to go on selling her the stuff. An hour later Mr. Trumbull burst into this office, put a gun in my face, and told me that I *would* sell her the stuff or he would kill me. I yielded. I think it was a wise decision, though I'm hardly proud of it.

"I'm telling you all this for a reason, Mr. Moreland. I have a certain amount of integrity as a physician. It's been strained over the years, but I cling to what's left of it. I'd rather you didn't think that I accepted favors from Vicki in exchange for laudanum. I didn't. She was a pathetic woman. She had beauty and talent and charm, but she was trapped in a web. People who are trapped become liars. At first it's a convenience, but gradually it becomes an instinct. She lied about me, and I would guess that she lied about you at one time or another."

Gil nodded. Gibson's story helped explain Vicki's entanglement with Trumbull. "Where is Trumbull? Have you heard anything about him?"

Gibson shook his head. "The soldiers went out looking for him after we got the news of the murders. They went through The Flat and made a halfhearted search of the surrounding country, but he had already escaped. I've heard that he went north—Kansas, maybe. He'll never be caught. If he had stolen five dollars from an officer, they would have tracked him down in a matter of days. But he merely murdered two people. Our post commander doesn't have time to attend to such trifles." He stood up, and Gil noticed that he was slow to put weight on his right foot. "May I examine the wild man? William, I believe you called him. Where did you get the name?"

Gil explained that if you shortened wild man to w.m., you had the abbreviated form of William. That name had seemed as good as any.

They went out into the hall. As soon as Gil opened the door, he walked into the stony yellow gaze, as though William had been staring at that very spot since Gil had left him there an hour ago.

Dr. Gibson was patient with William and spoke to him in a kind voice while he conducted his examination. Gil couldn't help smiling at this, since he recalled how gruff the doctor had been when *he* had come in the first time. William sat as stiff as a tree on the examining table, didn't utter a sound or show any expression on his face. When Gibson was through, he led William back out into the hall and told him to wait a few more minutes. He limped back into the office and closed the door.

"What do you know about William? Has he ever told you anything about his background?" Gil said that he knew almost nothing. Gibson dropped into his chair and lit another cigar. He held the match up and looked at it before he blew it out. "His eyes are the color of this flame. Very unusual. He doesn't come from conventional Indian stock. I've examined a lot of them—Tonkawas, Delawares, Caddos, Wichitas, Wacos, Tawakonis, and a few of the wild Comanches and Kiowas. William isn't one of those. He's much too large. He doesn't have the moon face or the high cheekbones, and his femur is much longer than an Indian's.

"And I'm fascinated by his teeth. The teeth of Indians usually begin to break down around the age of twenty-five or thirty. William's teeth are almost perfect. They're better than mine, probably better than yours. It almost makes one think that he knows something about the care of teeth and gums, something even we don't know about. You've uncovered a real mystery here. You said something about leaving him at the fort? What sort of thing did you have in mind?"

Gil told him about the troubles he had had with William. "I can't take him with me everywhere I go, but I don't dare leave him unattended. He's not entirely predictable. Sometimes I have to threaten to use force on him."

"I see." Gibson sat thinking for several minutes, drumming his fingers on the desk top. "I would be interested in keeping him for a while, just to satisfy my own curiosity. But this is a military garrison and there are limits to what I can do. If he stayed here, I would have to find a place for him. He would have to work, and I'm afraid the only job I could find for him would be the fatigue detail in the hospital."

He explained that the hospital detail was the most hated assignment at the fort. Nobody wanted hospital duty, which required that a man attend to the zinc-lined toilets that were wheeled through the ward to accommodate the patients. Twice a day, these "sinks" had to be cleaned and emptied, and the contents carted away from the fort.

"If you have no objections to William doing this sort of work, I can guarantee that no one will complain about his presence here." Gil said he had no objections. "And there's one more thing, Mr. Moreland. This may sound harsh to you, but I would have to insist that he be shackled."

"Shackled? You mean kept in chains?"

Gibson smiled. "Not exactly. Deserters awaiting court-martial or transfer are often fitted with a bar shackle that is fastened from one ankle to another. It would limit his movement, but it wouldn't be as severe as a ball and chain or a neck iron. I don't like the idea any more than you do, but please understand my position. I can't allow a wild man, or whatever he is now, on my wards without some sort of restraining device. If he caused mischief, I would be in a bad situation."

Gil thought it over and admitted that Gibson had no choice.

Gibson nodded. "We'll plan to keep him a month or two. I can't agree to anything beyond that. We'll have to see how things go."

They took William to the blacksmith shop and told him to sit down in a chair. The smith, a big, burly man who was stripped to the waist, brought a bar shackle out of a wooden chest and began sizing the ankle irons. Dr. Gibson did not watch but stood at the barn door, smoking and staring outside. Gil watched the smith and tried to avoid William's puzzled looks. William didn't understand what was going on or what the device would do to him.

The smith finished his work in half an hour. He rested his hammer on his shoulder, stood back, and in a rough tone of voice, told William to stand up. He came out of the chair and stared at the bar shackle. He tried to take a step and fell down. His eyes came up and locked on Gil. "No. No good, don't want."

The smith watched with a smirk. Gil walked over to Dr. Gibson. "Let me have a few minutes alone with William." Gibson nodded, called the blacksmith, and they went outside. William was on the ground, fighting the steel bands and trying to break them. Gil walked over to him.

"William, I have to go away for a while. I'm leaving you here with Dr. Gibson. He's a good man, he'll take care of you. I'm sorry about the shackle. It wasn't my idea, but you're just going to have to get used to it."

William's hands clawed at the device. When he saw that it was hopeless, he slumped back. "Bad, no good." His eyes came up. "Why?"

"Because nobody knows what to do with you, William, that's why. If I turned you loose, you'd be in the middle of a fight in half an hour. You'd probably get yourself killed. I know you can't help it. I can't help it, nobody can help it. That's just the way the world is. While I'm gone, you're going to help Dr. Gibson. Please don't make trouble. Do you understand?"

William glared up at him. "Vee-kee. Want Vee-kee."

"I'm sorry." He could think of nothing else to say. He called Dr. Gibson back in. Gibson went over and helped William to his feet. He held his arm while he learned to walk in the shackle, which kept his ankles spread about three feet apart. Gibson asked Gil to stay around for a while, and they returned to the hospital.

Gil waited near the door while Gibson led William onto the ward. Patients sat up in their beds and stared at the strange sight. Several of them grinned as William clanked past, and one, a large Negro soldier, called out something which Gil didn't hear.

But William heard. He stopped and glared at the man. Dr. Gibson stepped between them and steered William on to the far end of the ward, where three movable latrines stood near the back door. Gibson showed him how to remove the two zinc-lined drawers from the bottom of the device and dump the contents into a hogshead barrel that stood on a loading dock outside.

William caught on to the work quickly, and Dr. Gibson stood by while he did the next two drawers by himself. Then he slipped away and joined Gil.

"I think it's going to be all right. You can leave any time you wish."

Gil thanked him and told him where he could be reached in case of an emergency. "Dr. Gibson, is there a chance that you could wean him off the opium?"

Gibson was watching William. "We'll see. If all goes well for a few weeks, I'd like to try it." The patients had begun heckling William again. Dr. Gibson muttered an oath under his breath. "The idiots, don't they have anything better to do? You'd better go, Mr. Moreland. I'll take care of things. Don't worry. Good-bye."

At the door Gil looked back and saw that William was watching him. Gil lifted his hand and waved good-bye. William turned away.

Outside, he walked to the livery barn and filled his lungs with sweet spring air. His mind held a picture of William lumbering through the hospital in his shackles. When he climbed on Snip and rode east on the Weatherford road, the image was still there. But it was such a glorious day, and he felt so good about seeing Martha again, his thoughts about William began to fade.

For the first time in six months, the wild man was someone else's problem, and Gil felt as though a heavy weight had been lifted from his shoulders.

16

It was late in the afternoon of the following day when he rode into Weatherford. He passed the stone courthouse and studied the buildings on the town square. Nothing had changed. It was the same old town, but it looked better to him this time.

He headed for the Valkenburg mansion. Mrs. Valkenburg had told him that she would be sitting by the window watching for his return. He was curious to see if she was. He tied Snip to the hitching rail in front of the house, slacked his cinch, and walked up the stone steps to the yard gate. He paused there and looked up to his room on the second floor. Nothing had changed, only the season of the year. He heard the front door open and saw her coming out on the porch. She was smiling and her blue eyes shone with joy.

She was pale and thin, her hair the dull gray color of iron, and she was humped over a walking cane. Even at this distance he could see her gnarled fingers and swollen joints.

He ran up the walk, took the steps in two bounds, and wrapped his arms around her frail body. He caught the odor of her hair and her perfume, and it brought back warm memories of his childhood.

"Gil," she cried, "you've come home! I'm so glad to see you. Didn't I tell you I'd be watching out the window?"

Pearl, the Negro maid, came out the door. There was a storm of wrinkles on her brow. "Missa Falconbird, you know you not sposed to . . ." She saw Gil and her mouth fell open. "Well, lookie here what the dogs drug up. Mista Gil, you old rascal! Are you hongry?"

He gave Pearl a hug and told her that he was hungry enough to eat a small horse. She cackled and said she didn't have no horsemeat, but she could sure enough fry up some chicken.

They went inside, and while Pearl hurried off to the kitchen, Gil and Mrs. Valkenburg went into the library. It took her a long time to walk through the house. She had grown feeble.

They talked until supper. Gil told her about Phantom Hill and Fort Griffin, some of the people he had met and the places he had seen. He didn't mention anything about the wild man or Ben Woolsey's death. After supper, while Mrs. Valkenburg sipped on her evening glass of red wine, Gil helped Pearl clear the table. In the kitchen, he asked her about Mrs. Valkenburg's health.

"She got troubles." Pearl's eyes saddened and she shook her head. "Bad authoritus in her hands and knees, and the doctor say she got something wrong wid her heart. But she still have plenty of pluck, and"—she laughed—"she tearin' up all my nice floors wit that stick."

"Pearl, have you heard anything about Martha Wynn?"

Her big black eyes rolled around and fixed on him. "You ain't heard? She gonna marry that lawyer."

Gil's heart sank. "James Kennington?"

"Yeah, the one that ride them race horses. They tell me that she gonna make him give up the ponies, but he gonna ride right up to the day of the weddin'." She gave her head a toss. "I don't like her no more. She just like all them other silly girls 'round here, don't have dog sense when it come to pickin' a man."

"Well, I'm the one who called it off, Pearl. I can't blame Martha."

"Huh! I can. You be nice if you want, but I'm gonna"—she gave him a wicked scowl—"hold a *grudge.*"

Gil sat at the table talking with Mrs. Valkenburg until eight o'clock. When the grandfather clock chimed the hour, she pushed herself out of the chair and said good night. Pearl helped her into the bedroom, and Gil was alone with the ticking clock. He went up the stairs, took a bath and shaved, found a clean suit in his closet, and left the house at a quarter to nine. He had already put up Snip for the night, so he walked to the Wynn house.

A handsome one-horse carriage was parked in front of the house, and he knew that it must belong to James Kennington. It reflected what he knew about the man. It was sporty, well kept, and expensive. The horse was a dappled gray gelding with good strong lines, a fine head, and a slick coat that showed he had been well cared for. Gil almost turned around and left. He didn't want to see James Kennington or to intrude, but he found himself on the porch, knocking on the door.

Martha's mother was smiling when she opened the door. Her smile vanished when she saw Gil, and she stepped out on the porch and closed the door behind her.

"What do you want, Gil?"

"I just came to town this afternoon and I'd like to see Martha."

"She doesn't want to see you. She's going to be married to a fine man who will treat her well."

"I know that, Mrs. Wynn."

"Then why are you here? She doesn't need any more of

your kind of trouble. You've caused her enough grief, Gil Moreland. Please go away and leave us alone."

The door opened and Martha stepped out. "Mother? Who is . . ." A look of astonishment came to her face when she saw him. "Gil!"

Mrs. Wynn sighed and shook her head. "Well, it's none of my business." She was still muttering when she went into the house.

"Hello, Martha."

"Hello, Gil."

"You didn't answer my letters."

She dropped her eyes. "Come inside, Gil. I want you to meet James."

The last time Gil had seen Kennington, he had been a tall, awkward boy who was either doting over his horses or reading a book. When he rose from his chair, Gil could see that he had filled out in his chest and shoulders. He sported a rakish mustache, every bit as flamboyant as Gil's, and his eyes beamed with strength and confidence.

"James, you remember Gil Moreland."

"Yes, of course." Kennington offered his hand and gave Gil's a hard squeeze, a bit harder than necessary, Gil thought. "I understand you've been to the frontier. I envy you. I've always dreamed of going, but one can't do everything." He gave Gil a pleasant smile and lifted one brow. "I'll be going now, Martha."

"Oh no, please don't go, James."

"It's late, dear, and I have a race at six o'clock in the morning. Ollie Benton and I are going to match our mares on the half mile. And I'm sure you old friends will have a lot to talk about." He turned to Gil. There was no malice or jealousy in his face. He seemed very sure of his place in Martha's life, almost cocky. "Good night, Gil. You'll probably be leaving soon, so if I don't see you again, best of luck to you. And Martha, I'll see you for lunch tomorrow."

"Oh . . . yes, lunch." She walked him to the door. "James, please be careful. When you get on those horses, you seem to throw caution to the wind."

He answered her with a laugh, and a moment later they heard his carriage pull away. Their eyes met and Gil tried to read her face. He decided that she was not happy to see him. She seemed almost afraid of him.

They stood in the living room, and neither could think of anything to say. Gil was aware of Mrs. Wynn's presence in the house, for although she had left the room, he could hear her banging and bumping things at the back of the house. No accident, he was sure.

"Could we go out on the porch?" he asked.

She hesitated and glanced over her shoulder. "I guess it would be all right, but not for long."

Out on the porch she kept her distance from him and stood in a rigid pose with her hands clasped in front of her. She gazed out at the moonlit lawn. "Why did you have to come back?" she asked, just above a whisper.

"I've thought about you a great deal, Martha."

"Have you?"

"Why didn't you answer my letters?"

"I had nothing to say. And"—her head snapped around—"why didn't you answer *mine?* I swallowed my pride and wrote you a long letter, and then I waited at the mailbox every day for your reply. And every time I returned empty-handed, I had to face Mother's rebuking glare. 'Why are you waiting around for him?' she asked with her eyes. 'He had his chance, and he left.' "

"I know it sounds like a feeble excuse," he said, "but I tried to write you. I started a letter several times, but each time something came up and I didn't have a chance to finish it. Here." He reached into his pocket and pulled out four pages he had written back in September, only a few days after he had received her letter.

At first she didn't take it, but he insisted. She took it and went over to the window. Enough light was coming from inside the house so that she could read. She read it slowly, and the stern expression on her face did not change. When she came to the end, she looked up.

"Is this true, about the wild man?"

"It's true." He went on to tell her the whole story, about Vicki the Red, the capture of the wild man, the murders, the long winter he had spent with William, and the troubles that had forced him to leave William at Fort Griffin. He hadn't intended to tell her everything about Vicki, but it all came out. After all, what did he have to lose by telling the truth?

In the middle of his story, Mrs. Wynn stuck her head out the door and said, "Martha, it's *very* late and we have a lot to do tomorrow."

"Thank you, Mother. I'll come in when I'm ready. Go on with your story, Gil."

The door slammed, and they saw no more of Mrs. Wynn.

It must have been close to eleven o'clock when he finished. Once started, the story unraveled like a big ball of string. It was the first time he had had a chance to talk to anyone about it.

"That's a powerful story," she said, "almost a parable. Vicki came to a tragic end, but she seemed to have been looking for it. It's sad about the wild man, though. He didn't deserve what he got. His only crime was that he happened to step into the path of civilization. What will you do with him?"

Gil was sitting on the step. He picked up some pebbles and tossed them out into the yard. "I don't know what to do, Martha. It all started out as a lark, a kind of sporting event. I wanted to capture him just to see if I could do it, the way a kid traps a squirrel so that he can put him in a cage and watch him. But with William, it's become very complicated. I took him out of his world and brought him into mine." He looked up at her. "And Martha, there's no place for him in my world. I had my fun and I don't want him anymore. Nobody wants him." He noticed that she was smiling. "Did I say something funny?"

She brushed a wisp of hair away from her forehead and looked away. "William and I have something in common. You left me to go chase him. Now you're tired of that, and you've come back here. You have a way of blundering through life and stepping all over people's feelings, Gil. It makes me wonder if you have any feelings of your own."

Their eyes met. "I do have feelings, Martha. I've made some mistakes, but I had to make them. I wish we could start all over again."

"But we can't."

"Why?"

"Because we made our choices and now we have to live with them. You chose to go looking for adventure. You found plenty of it and I'm happy for you. But I chose not to wait around for your return."

"I wasn't ready for you then. I think I am now. I've changed, I've learned something about the world."

"You learned too late, Gil. I'm sorry."

He stood up and took her hands. She tried to pull away from him, but he held her. "It's not too late. You don't want to marry Kennington. You said so in your letter, and I saw it in your eyes tonight. I know you don't love him."

She glared at him. "No, I don't, but it doesn't matter anymore. I'm not looking for love. I'm willing to settle for less, just as my mother did, and her mother, and her mother. We do what we have to do to get a home and children. That's the way God intended it to be, and that's enough."

"I can give you a home and children."

"Can you? The kind of home you gave William?"

The remark went through him like a sword thrust. "That's different."

She jerked her hands away from him. "It's not different. You reveal yourself through what you do, not what you say. What you did to that poor man is what you would do to a wife: conquer and leave. That's not good enough for me, sorry. James will marry me, but he won't conquer me or leave me."

"Don't marry him."

"How dare you tell me what to do?"

"Don't marry him."

She stamped her foot. "I *will* marry him!"

"No you won't. I won't let you. I'll tie up Kennington and throw him on a baggage car bound for Mexico."

"Please leave. If you don't, I'll call Daddy."

"Call him, and when he comes out here, I'll stuff him into that rose bush. And I'll stuff your old lady right on top of him. I won't let you ruin our lives."

Her head fell down against her chest and she moaned. "Gil, please go away and leave me alone. Let me find a little bit of happiness. Think of someone besides yourself, just this once. I beg you."

"I'm thinking of both of us. I won't let you marry Kennington. I'm going now, but I'll be back. Good night, Martha." She stood with her back to him and didn't respond. He hurried down the flagstone walk. At the yard gate, he looked back at her. She had not moved.

All the way back to the house he felt light-headed and giddy. He had gone to Martha's house without knowing what he would say to her, yet somehow, through blind luck or instinct, it had all come out right. All at once his mind was clear. He knew that he wanted her. If James Kennington tried to stand in the way, he would learn something that couldn't be found in his law books. Poor Kennington. This was one horse race he would lose.

It was past midnight when he crawled into bed. For a long time he lay awake, listening to the crickets and thinking about Martha. He had caused her a lot of pain, but he would make it up to her. He would be kind and gentle, he would make her happy. He wouldn't move her into the house with Mrs. Valkenburg. She would need a house of her own. They would build one on the edge of town, with plenty of space for dogs and children. He fell into a peaceful sleep and did not stir all night.

He heard a knock at the door. He opened his eyes and looked around, trying to remember where he was. It was morning, and he still felt the warmth of pleasant dreams.

"Mista Gil, Mista Gil." Pearl was pounding on the door. "Wake up, you got a telegram."

He jumped out of bed, threw on a robe, and opened the door. Pearl handed him the telegram and told him that his breakfast would be ready in ten minutes. He muttered a thank you and sat down on the edge of the bed. He stared at the unopened telegram. It had to be from Dr. Gibson, and it could hold nothing but bad news. He didn't want to read it. He threw it into the trash basket, dressed, and went down for breakfast.

At the table he picked at his pancakes and ham while Pearl hovered nearby, ostensibly dusting the china cabinet but actually watching him. Finally, she slapped her hands on her hips and gave him one of her patented scowls, with her lips pooched out and her brow corrugated with wrinkles.

"What's wrong wit you? Ain't no pizon on that plate. I spend all mornin' fixin' a big breckfuss and don't nobody in this house want to eat. Missa Falconbird eat the same way—pick, pick, pick—then send most of it back for the cats."

Gil was lost in thought and hardly heard her. He laid down his fork and got up from the table. "I'm sorry, Pearl, I'm just not hungry."

He left the room and heard her grumble, "Well, skee-use *me!*"

He ran up the stairs and into his room. He picked the telegram out of the trash and held it up. He tore it open and read:

GIL MORELAND
WEATHERFORD, TEXAS

MR MORELAND WM KILLED SOLDIER THIS PM ESCAPED TRACKED DOWN APPREHENDED NOW IN GUARDHOUSE AWAITING EXECUTION URGENT YOU COME AT ONCE

DR GIBSON
FORT GRIFFIN TEXAS

The telegram fell from his fingers. "Oh, God no, not now." He slumped down onto the edge of the bed and stared at the wall. Down below he heard the clock chime the quarter hour and then the half hour. He stood up, found a sheet of paper and a pen, and began writing.

Dearest Martha:

Enclosed is a telegram I received this morning. I am crushed by this news. I do not want to go but I must, to bring

the problem I created to a solution. I will return to you, in days, weeks, or months, whatever is required. I want to marry you. Please wait. Enclosed you will find my mother's wedding band. I hope you will wear it.

Affectionately,
GIL

17

When Dr. Gibson saw him step onto the hospital ward, he finished his conversation with a young trooper and came to the door, walking with long strides and with his head down. He stripped off his white hospital gown and hung it on a peg by the door.

"Mr. Moreland, I'm glad you came at once. We haven't a moment to spare. Let's go outside where we can talk."

He swept out the door and Gil fell in step beside him, and soon discovered that he walked at a brisk pace. He fumbled through his pockets until he found the two-inch butt of one of his thin cigars. He stopped to light it, inhaled the smoke, and resumed his fast walk. He had dark rings under his eyes and he looked weary. They had gone several hundred yards before he spoke.

"I never should have agreed to keep your man. I underestimated the problems. I'm not blaming you. It's my fault.

"Let me tell you briefly what happened. Do you remember the big soldier who was on the ward the day you were here, the one who was heckling William? That was Private Garwood, a chronic fighter and troublemaker. He was in the hospital with a case of severe alcoholism. He had no business there. He should have been in the guardhouse. He had the sure instincts of a bully, and apparently he sensed some weakness in William. There was conflict between them the instant they laid eyes on each other.

"Private Garwood missed no opportunity to torment William. He had no pain or sickness to occupy his mind, so he had nothing better to do than agitate. He got some of the other patients involved. Every time William walked past, they would whistle at him and throw things. I saw what was happening and tried to nip it in the bud. I told Garwood that if he kept it up, I would have him transferred to the guardhouse. That was no threat to him. He had spent half his tour in the guardhouse. He kept it up.

"I must say that William showed restraint. You could tell that it bothered him, but he kept his head and didn't do anything—until the day after you left. It was around three o'clock in the afternoon. He was pushing one of the toilets to the back of the ward. Apparently, Garwood had found a crutch somewhere, and when William walked past his bed, he pushed it out into the aisle and tripped him. William fell hard. Wearing the shackle, he couldn't keep his balance.

"Everyone on the ward had been watching, and when he fell, there was an explosion of laughter. I was in my office and heard it. I thought nothing of it. Minutes later, I heard a general uproar, and one of the nurses rushed in and said that a fight was on. By the time I reached the ward, it was already over. Garwood lay dead on the floor, and William had fled out the back door. Garwood's skull had been crushed by a blow from a hammer."

"Where did he get a hammer?"

"I don't know. He must have found it lying around somewhere earlier in the day and concealed it in his clothing. I would guess that he was afraid of Garwood—most people were—and decided to carry it for protection. When the time came, he had it and used it.

"A mounted patrol went out within the hour. They took

several trail hounds and captured him about three miles north of here. They brought him back, he was clapped into irons and locked in the guardhouse. He's there now. Unless something is done soon, he'll probably be hanged within three days."

"What can be done?"

Gibson stopped in the shade of a pecan tree. They were well outside the perimeter of the fort now, and he glanced around to make sure they were alone.

"I've discussed the case with Commander Newsome. I managed to convince him that the cause of justice has already been served, and that hanging William would merely be a blot on our record. He agrees, but he's in an awkward position. He can hardly condone the killing of a soldier by a civilian, and then there is the matter of race. Garwood was a Negro, as are most of the troopers here. He had friends, and they might make a racial issue out of it. Commander Newsome wants the matter ended without any more bloodshed or trouble."

Gibson pulled a set of keys out of his pocket. "Newsome's last word to me was that he could do nothing to help William. As he said that, he handed me these keys. The next step is up to you, Mr. Moreland. The guard is changed at nine o'clock. There is a period of ten to fifteen minutes when the guardhouse is unattended. If you want to save William, I suggest you move tonight. I'll do whatever I can to help with the preparations. *But"*—he aimed a finger at Gil—"if the plot fails and you're caught, you'll have to stand alone and take the consequences. Newsome and I will disavow you. We'll have no choice. What do you say?"

Gil thought it over and considered all the possibilities. "I brought him here. I can't just throw him to the dogs."

Gibson pressed his lips together and nodded. "I hoped

you would see it that way." He glanced up at the sun. "We don't have much time. Here is the plan I've worked out."

Around sundown, Gil walked up Government Hill and hid in a small barn behind Dr. Gibson's house. At eight-thirty Gibson appeared, leading Snip, a second saddle horse, and a packhorse loaded with supplies for the trip. He gave Gil the keys: one for the cell door, one for the neck iron, and one for the ankle shackles.

All of a sudden, Gil was struck by a thought. "We forgot about laudanum. I don't have any. I left it all with you."

A sad smile tugged at Gibson's mouth. "I've packed you a two-month supply in pint bottles. That will be enough to get you through to Kansas. After that, you're on your own." He offered his hand. "Good luck, Mr. Moreland."

At five minutes to nine, Gil left the barn and slipped through the shadows until he reached the forage house near the southwest corner of the fort. From here he could see the guardhouse, four stone cells sitting in a row off to themselves. He could see the guard pacing around, carrying his carbine in the crook of his arm. The guard yawned and pulled a watch out of his pocket and held it up to the moonlight. He took one last look around and started walking toward company quarters.

Gil waited a minute or two, then ran across the open field to the guardhouse. He fitted the big key into the lock, turned it and opened the door. He could just barely make out the dark form of William lying on the straw. He called his name and William sat up.

"William, I've come to help you. Don't be afraid."

"Gil!" he cried, and jumped to his feet, causing his chains to clank and rattle.

"Shhh! Don't make a sound." He stepped inside the cell and was smothered in an embrace. It took him half a minute to pry himself out of William's grasp. His hands were trembling so badly by this time that he couldn't fit the key into the neck iron. But at last it slipped into the hole and the big iron fell to the floor. He unlocked the ankle shackles, closed and locked the cell door behind them, and headed for the forage house. William was right beside him. Gil could see the night guard walking from company quarters. He carried his carbine over his shoulder and was whistling a tune.

They didn't have a minute to lose. They ran all the way to Gibson's barn and climbed on the horses. They rode quietly through the fort, heading north. Once past the bakery and the adjutant's office, there was nothing between them and Kansas but a sea of prairie grass. Gil checked the north star and set their course to the northeast, toward Buzzard Peak on the edge of the gypsum belt in the Pease River country. He loped out. With luck, they would be there in two days. It was unlikely that the soldiers would follow them into the gypsum belt.

They rode all night, making good time in the cool air. At daybreak they stopped and slept for several hours while the horses grazed nearby on good grass. Before noon they pushed on. By nightfall they could see Buzzard Peak in the distance. Throughout the afternoon Gil had looked back over their trail expecting to see a cloud of dust rising over a column of blue riders. But he had seen nothing.

William had hardly spoken a word since the escape, but that night, as they prepared for sleep, he pointed toward the north and said, "Home."

Gil had felt secure enough to build a small fire and was drinking coffee. Bless him, Dr. Gibson must have known that even when a man was fleeing from the United States Army he needed a good strong cup of Arbuckle's coffee. "What do you mean?"

William pointed north again and said, "Home."

"Whose home?"

He pointed to himself. "William home."

"Home" was not a word William had ever used before, nor had he ever revealed anything about his past. Gil pressed him for details but learned very little. As he understood it, William was saying that he had spent his childhood somewhere to the north. And he seemed to think that's where they were going. Gil was curious about this and kept asking questions, but William had said all he wanted to say, and he ended the conversation as abruptly as he had begun it. He asked for red water. Shortly after he drank the laudanum, he fell asleep.

The next morning Gil filled the canteens with fresh water. They would need all the water they could carry, because ahead of them lay the gypsum belt. Gil had never passed through this country before, but he had heard Ben Woolsey talk about it. What water you could find in this wasteland was likely to be poisonous.

As he pushed the first canteen under the water, he happened to glance off to the south and saw a plume of dust rising over a column of riders.

He leaped to his feet. "William, the soldiers are coming! Saddle the horses, we've got to get out of here!"

William looked toward the dust cloud, pressed his lips together, and went to work saddling the horses. Gil grabbed everything in sight—pots, pans, clothes—and stuffed them into the pack. What he could not stuff into the pack, he left behind. They leaped into their saddles and galloped off to the north, toward the gypsum belt.

They had been on the trail an hour or more when Gil glanced down at the saddle horn, where he kept his canteen, and saw that it was not there. He let out a cry. He had left both canteens beside the spring!

Before long, the terrain became broken, rugged, and desolate. They rode through deep arroyos and across wide, flat expanses where the red earth had been baked and cracked by the sun. They passed a few holes where the water was gray with gypsum. Beside several of these, the bones of dead animals lay baking in the hot sun. Gil kept throwing glances over his shoulder.

The dust cloud was still following them. The soldiers had not turned back at the edge of the gypsum belt. Looking up ahead, he saw the same desolation they had passed through for hours. He licked his lips. He was beginning to suffer from thirst. He told William about the canteens. The stony face showed nothing, not fear, not anger, nothing.

They rode on. The cool of morning gave way to brutal heat. The air was hot and still, and heat rose from the ground. The cloud of red dust was still behind them. By the middle of the afternoon, the horses had slowed to a walk. No amount of spurring could coax them into a trot. Darkness fell, but they did not dare stop.

William was riding in the lead now. Gil was so tired and weak from thirst that he no longer cared where they were going. He dozed off, lulled by the rocking motion of the horse. Once, when he awoke, he looked up at the sky and found the North Star. They were no longer heading due north. William must have lost his bearings.

The next time Gil opened his eyes, he saw the first light of dawn on the eastern horizon. The brilliant red sky reminded him of a hot iron or a brick oven. He turned around in the saddle and looked back to the south. The dust cloud was gone. They had escaped the cavalry, only to find themselves out in the middle of an arid wasteland. William was still riding in the lead, and his posture in the saddle indicated that he too was suffering from fatigue and thirst. But he seemed to know where he was going. If he didn't, if they were traveling in a circle, they would both be dead in a matter of days.

As the day heated up, Gil drifted off into a half sleep that was haunted with dreams of devils and animals. All at once Snip stopped, and Gil opened his eyes. He saw a pool of water in front of him. It stood beneath a rock ledge, and several big mesquite trees cast their shade over it. He heard his mouth crackle as he licked his lips. He could almost taste the water. It *had* to be good water. Surely it came from a spring that gushed out of the rocks.

He jumped off his horse and started running. Just before he got there, he felt a big hand close around his shoulder. He turned around and looked into William's eyes. "Let me go. I've got to have a drink."

"Bad water."

"It's good water, I can tell. See how clear it is? You can see the bottom. Let me go!"

He struggled and broke away from William's grip. Only two more steps and he could end the burning in his mouth and throat. William caught him at the pool's edge, threw both arms around his neck, and wrestled him to the ground. Gil fought back. He couldn't understand why William was doing this. He had to drink!

"Bad water, make die, not for drink."

Gil stopped struggling and lay there for a moment, blinking his eyes and panting for breath. The sun burned white hot in the sky. He could feel it searing his skin. William was sitting on his abdomen and had pinned his arms to the ground. William had overpowered him and had gained the upper hand. If William wanted to kill him, he could do it. Nobody would find the bones. Nobody would ever know.

He closed his eyes against the glare and let his lungs fight for air. Slowly, he began to realize that he had gone out of his head from the heat and thirst.

"I think I'll be all right now, William. You're smashing

me. Would you get off, please?" William stood up. "I won't drink, but let me wash my face."

William shook his head and stepped between Gil and the water. "Bad water for Gil. Good water"—he pointed to the northeast—"there. Wait."

Gil tried to swallow. His saliva was as thick as paste. "Would you let me soak my feet?" William shook his head. "You don't trust my willpower, do you? Neither do I."

He staggered to his horse and pulled himself into the saddle. William rode in the lead. Now and then, he glanced over his shoulder to make sure Gil had not gone back.

"You don't need to check on me," Gil muttered. "I'm not a child."

He closed his eyes, slumped over the fork of the saddle, and drifted into a fitful doze. The hours dragged by as he bobbed up and down in time with Snip's slow walk. Then the horse stopped. Gil opened his eyes and tried to focus. His head was reeling. He felt himself falling out of the saddle, but when he tried to catch his balance, he discovered that his body would not respond. His feet didn't touch the ground. Where was the ground? He seemed to be floating through the air. A familiar musky smell filled his nostrils. His vision began to clear, and he found himself looking straight into William's yellow eyes.

"What are you doing to me?"

William carried him to the edge of a pool and threw him in. The cool water closed around him and brought him blessed relief. He drank and washed his face, drank some more and rubbed the water on his parched lips. He saw the necks of the horses bend to the water's edge as they drank. William knelt on the sandy bank, drinking from the cup of his hand. Gil crawled to the shallow water near the bank and lay on his back, listening to the clatter of the cottonwood leaves as life returned to his body.

When he was strong enough to stand, he saw that William had started a fire and made camp. Gil walked up to him and laid a hand on his shoulder.

"Thanks, my friend."

William almost smiled. "Good water."

"The best water on God's earth."

William pointed to the north, and for the first time, Gil noticed that they had left the harsh and jagged terrain behind them. To the north the green shortgrass prairie rolled as far as the eye could see. "Home," said William.

There was just a hint of delight in his face, something Gil had not seen before. "You take us to this home of yours. I want to see it."

18

The next day they traveled at a leisurely pace. William rode in front and set the course due north. At dusk they made their camp near a creek of clear water. Gil shot a wild turkey off its roost in a big cottonwood, and they stuffed themselves on the lean, dark meat which they roasted over coals of cottonwood bark.

Just before darkness fell he brought out a map that Dr. Gibson had given him. It was a military campaign map that showed the routes taken by several expeditions that had crossed the Panhandle region. He could only guess where they were now, and his best guess placed them on the Washita River, about thirty miles south of the Canadian River. Kansas lay a hundred and fifty miles to the north.

Kansas was a new country, trying to build itself on the edge of the frontier. People there didn't care where a man came from or what he had done in his past. Maybe William could find a job, make a place for himself, and get a fresh start.

William was looking at him. "Red water."

There was the problem. How could a man addicted to opium make his way in the world? William had problems enough with language and his bizarre appearance. His addiction made him hopelessly dependent and vulnerable.

"William, you must stop taking the red water."

"Want red water."

"I know you want it, but it's bad. It's bad water."

William shook his head. "Good. Want red water."

"If it's good, why don't *I* drink it?"

How could he explain drug addiction to this man? He wasn't sure it could be done, but he decided to try. He talked for an hour or more, using the primitive vocabulary they had developed. It finally occurred to him to use the imagery of a trap to describe the laudanum. William knew about traps. It was something he understood. Gil talked until his throat was sore. He had no idea how much of it William absorbed, since his face was as blank as a slab of rock.

"Want red water."

Gil sighed. "All right, I'll give it to you one more time. But when we reach this home you keep talking about, no more red water."

"Home. No more red water." He said the words, but whether he understood them, Gil didn't know.

He poured the laudanum into the cup and William gulped it down. Minutes later his head began to drop toward his chest. His lids drooped over his eyes, and he drifted off into a sleep.

They got an early start the next morning. William seemed anxious to move on, and several times during the day Gil had to kick old Snip into a lope to catch up with him. They crossed the Canadian River around the middle of the afternoon. They were fortunate that this treacherous stream was not in flood or boggy with quicksand. On the north bank William changed his course and headed toward some deep canyons that lay five miles to the northwest. He no longer trotted his horse, but kicked him up into a lope. Gil came along behind, slowed by the packhorse.

They struck a dry streambed, and here William turned back to the north, following the stream into a wide valley. As they moved further north, it narrowed, and the walls on both sides rose higher. The valley became a canyon, surrounded by walls of sheer white rock. Around dusk William pointed to a tall, cone-shaped hill in the middle of the canyon. He turned around in the saddle and cried, "Home!" His eyes were glistening. He dug his heels into his horse and galloped ahead. Gil followed as fast as he could.

William disappeared behind some rocks, and Gil lost sight of him for ten or fifteen minutes. Then, as he rode around a bend in the stream, what he saw ahead of him made him stare in wonder. There, in the bottom of the canyon, was a small city, with one- and two-story dwellings made of white rock. Some of the buildings were in ruins, while others were intact. The whole area around the city was overgrown with weeds and grass. The town was abandoned.

William stood in front of one of the dwellings. His head was thrown back, and he reached out to it with his arms spread wide apart. As Gil rode up, he dropped to his knees and bent his head to the ground. Gil stepped out of the saddle and walked toward him.

A light evening breeze moaned through the stone walls. Above that there was not a sound in the world. The canyon held an awesome silence. Gil waited and watched. He heard a muffled cry. William's body was trembling. He dug his hands into the soil, raised up from the kneeling position, and let the earth fall through his fingers. He stood up, and when he turned to Gil, his eyes were filled with tears.

"Home," he cried. "William home here. Little boy here. Home."

William had finally found his place. He had found his past and his source, a stone city that appeared to have been abandoned half a century ago. Where had these people gone, why had they left? The stone walls were golden now in the last rays of the sun, the color of William's eyes.

While William walked around the ruins, Gil unsaddled the horses and put them out on a flat of good grass. He could see that the afternoon's fast pace had left them tired. They would need several days' rest.

He moved the gear and equipment into one of the buildings which appeared to be solid. He made a fire in the stone fireplace, boiled some coffee, and put some dried beans on to cook. Darkness fell. An owl hooted somewhere nearby, and out on the prairie coyotes sang a mournful chorus that lasted several minutes and then stopped, as if on command. Now and then, he heard William's steps as he continued to prowl through the buildings. Gil left him alone, drank coffee, and stared into the fire.

Whoever these people were, they had been exceptional stonemasons. They had laid up walls of solid rock and had used no mortar, yet every wall was square and plumb. They had even left air vents so that a cool south breeze could pass through the room.

It was near ten o'clock when William returned. He squatted down on the floor and was silent for a while. Then he tried to tell Gil about his home.

They were peaceful people, he said, farmers who diverted spring water and rain water to irrigate crops of pumpkins, beans, corn, and—unless Gil misunderstood the gesture of a man smoking a pipe—tobacco. They hunted small game with bows and arrows, wove baskets, and made pottery from clay dug out of the riverbed.

William acted out a battle with spears, clubs, and bows and arrows. Many years ago the town was attacked by a warlike people from the west. Most of the villagers were either killed or carried off into slavery, but some were able to escape and hide in the canyons. When the attackers left, these people returned to their homes. Among them were William's ancestors. Since the attackers had destroyed the crops, they suffered through a winter of hunger and disease, but a remnant of strong ones survived, planted crops again in the spring, and began to prosper.

Then, when William was a small boy, the city was attacked again, this time by Comanches. They seemed to come out of nowhere, like lightning out of a clear sky. Mounted on ponies, they came thundering up the valley and caught the villagers by surprise. The canyon, which had seemed to make the village invulnerable to attack, became a death trap. The Comanches chased the villagers to the sheer walls at the head of the canyon and then killed them like rats. No one was spared. The Comanches pillaged the town, stole what they wanted, and destroyed what they didn't want.

"How did you escape?" Gil asked.

William pointed to the cone-shaped hill that stood just south of the village. He was five years old at the time and had been assigned the duty of lookout. Since the city had not been attacked in many years, the sentry job was foisted off on children. It was tedious, and the men preferred to hunt or work in the fields. But it was just as tedious for the children, and on that fateful day, when the Comanches came pouring into the canyon, William was chasing lizards. By the time he saw the Comanches, it was too late to sound the alarm. He hid in the rocks and watched the Comanches destroy his people.

"How did you survive?" Gil asked.

William pointed to the south and said that he began walking, drifting with the winds. He lived on roots, berries, leaves, insects, anything he could find. By the next spring, his clothes had fallen away and he had forgotten how to speak his native tongue. Then one day he discovered that wild animals were not afraid of him. They came right up to him, and some brought him food. He found that he could communicate with them, not with words but through some medium he didn't understand. The animals adopted him and taught him how to survive in the winter, where to find food. He grew into manhood, forgot his past, and thought of himself as an animal.

He paused and looked at Gil with bewildered eyes. "Who am I now?" he seemed to say. "My people are gone. The animals run away from me and your people despise me. Why did Vee-kee do this to me?"

They stared into the fire for a while, then William rolled up in a blanket and went to sleep in the corner. Gil pulled a small object out of his vest pocket and turned it over in his fingers. He had found it on the floor while he was cooking supper. It was a linen cartridge from a .52 caliber Sharps rifle, the standard weapon used by buffalo hunters.

Someone had camped within these walls, and not so very long ago. He had never heard of any buffalo hunting in this region, and he knew that the Medicine Lodge Treaty had declared it off limits to white hunters. But white hunters had come. Indians of the plains did not carry Sharps weapons.

He threw a big hardwood log on the fire, rolled up in his blanket, and drifted off to sleep. He had not been asleep very long when he awoke with a jolt.

It suddenly occurred to him that William had gone to bed without asking for laudanum.

They didn't have to wait long to see the first symptoms of withdrawal. By noon the next day William had begun to sweat and shiver. He couldn't sit still, and he paced and prowled the ruins. By the middle of the afternoon his nose and eyes were flowing, and he yawned continuously as though he couldn't breathe. That night Gil covered him with blankets and built a big fire, yet he shivered so hard that his teeth chattered.

The next morning his flesh was cold to the touch, his eyes were dilated, and his nose poured mucus. Gil fed him some hot broth, but no sooner did it hit his stomach than it came back up. By the third morning his stomach was contracting violently. His intestines writhed like snakes beneath his skin, and blood appeared in his vomit. That night he was seized by terrible chills that caused his whole body to shake. Gil covered him with blankets, saddle blankets, spare clothes, everything he could find, and within an hour the blankets were soaked with sweat.

On the fourth day both of them were exhausted. Gil had not gotten a full night's sleep since the ordeal began, and he had hardly left the house. Unable to keep anything in his stomach, William had grown so weak that he could hardly sit up. His eyes had become empty holes, ringed with dark circles, and his ribs showed beneath his skin. He was out of his head most of the time. He begged Gil to shoot him and put him out of his misery. He raved and screamed, his eyes so wild that they hardly seemed human. He cursed Vicki. He cursed Gil. He cried for the animals to help him. Then he seized Gil by the shirt and pleaded with him to give him some laudanum.

Through this dark period, Gil sat beside him, holding his hand and wiping his brow with a wet cloth. "Hang on just a little longer," he kept saying. "We've gone this far, let's don't give up. You've seen the worst of it."

But they hadn't seen the worst of it. That night William wept as muscle cramps seized his abdomen. He babbled incoherently, often using words that Gil didn't recognize. By midnight, his skin was gray and clammy. His eyes rolled back in his head and he went into convulsions. Gil thought he was dying. He couldn't stand to watch him suffer any longer.

He took William's head into his arms and gazed into his ravaged face. "I'm sorry, my friend. We've been beaten. God help me for what I'm going to do." He put a bottle of laudanum to William's mouth and forced the liquid down his throat.

The change was miraculous. Within half an hour, the convulsions ceased and William fell into a deep sleep, his first peaceful sleep in five days. Gil collapsed on the floor, prayed for forgiveness, and drifted into the numbing peace of sleep.

William recovered quickly. The color returned to his face and he began to gain back the weight he had lost. Two weeks after the ordeal began, he appeared to have made a full recovery.

But Gil noticed a change in his attitude. They hardly spoke to each other now, and it was nothing unusual for days to pass without a single word of communication between them. Gil tried to talk to him, but he wouldn't respond. There was a faraway look in his eyes and an air of sadness about him. When he was strong enough to walk, he left the house in the morning and returned at night, took his laudanum, and fell into a sleep.

Gil didn't know where he went during the day until one day he heard an odd sound, almost like music. He walked outside and listened. It *was* music, flute music. He followed the sound to the base of the lookout mountain. He climbed to the top and saw William sitting cross-legged, facing the south and playing Chopin on Vicki's recorder.

When he returned to the house that night, Gil gave him a plate of fried rabbit and beans. William ate it in a mechanical manner, as though he were merely throwing fodder to his body. He set his plate down and asked for red water. Gil had decided it was time for a talk.

"William, we've been here for three weeks. I think it's time for us to leave. We can be in Kansas in five days. We'll find a place for you."

He looked at Gil for a long time and shook his head. "Gil go. I stay. Home this place. Not leave."

"I can't leave you here. How would you live, what would you eat?"

"Animals help."

"No they won't. They're afraid of you."

"William stay."

Gil tried to argue with him, but William had made up his mind and there was no changing it. He asked for his red water and went to sleep. Gil stayed awake thinking. If William stayed, he would run out of laudanum in a month. He couldn't survive the withdrawal period without help. To leave him in the canyon was to leave him to die.

The next morning Gil tried again to persuade him to go to Kansas. William listened, shook his head, and walked out the door.

There was nothing left to say. Gil spent the day preparing for the long trip back to Weatherford. He hoped that Martha would be waiting.

19

At dawn they said good-bye. A strong south wind was whipping up through the valley. It moaned in the rock walls and rustled William's hair, which was growing long again.

Gil offered to divide up the supplies and leave William a horse and a pistol, but he refused, saying he didn't want them or need them. They stood in front of the stone house and looked at each other for the last time. In the morning light, William's eyes were golden.

"William, I don't know what to say to you. The things that come to mind sound trivial. They don't convey the feelings one has. I . . ." Tears came to his eyes as he looked at the big man in front of him. He threw his arms around him and held him in a tight embrace. "God bless you, William. I'm sorry for whatever cruelty I've done to you." He stepped back and wiped the tears from his eyes. "Good-bye, my friend."

They shook hands. Gil climbed on Snip and, leading the packhorse, started down the canyon. When he had gone a mile, he stopped and looked back. He could see William standing on top of the lookout mountain. He waved, and William raised his arm in farewell.

Following the dry streambed, he rounded a bend when all at once Snip let out a whinny. It was answered by another horse somewhere up ahead. Gil stopped and studied the terrain. This country still belonged to the Kiowas and Comanches, and he feared he might have blundered into an ambush. He pulled his pistol, listened, and watched.

Then he saw two men about two hundred yards away. They had already seen him. They were stopped, watching. They wore wide-brimmed hats and hunting shirts. They must be buffalo hunters. He breathed easier and raised his arm in a greeting.

"Hello there!" he called. His voice echoed through the canyon.

The larger of the two men raised his arm and waved back. "Who goes there?" he called.

"A friend." Gil holstered his pistol and rode toward them.

"Hold it where you are!" the man called out. Gil stopped. "Give your name."

They were a hundred yards away now, and he noticed for the first time that both men had drawn their rifles. He couldn't see much of them, only that one was heavyset and bearded, while the other was rather skinny.

"Gil Moreland!" he shouted. When the echoes died, he was astonished to hear the men laughing. "Who are you?"

There was a moment of silence, and then he heard one word echoing through the canyon. "Trumbull, Trumbull, Trumbull, Trumbull, Trumbull!"

He turned Snip, dug the spurs into his sides, and galloped back up the canyon. He heard the snap of a rifle shot and the hum of a bullet. He pulled his pistol and fired off two shots, lay flat along Snip's back, and urged him on with spurs. When he glanced back over his shoulder, he saw them coming after him.

He flew up the canyon, pushing Snip to his limits. The two men followed along at a distance. They didn't seem to be in any hurry to catch him. They must have known that there was only one way out of the canyon. Gil could see the lookout mountain up ahead, and on the very top of it he could barely make out the silhouette of William.

Gil waved his arms to give the alarm. He saw William stand up and then disappear. Gil pointed Snip toward the stone walls and urged him on. Only another three hundred yards. Snip was heaving for breath. The long dash through the sand had sapped his energy. Gil spurred hard, but the horse was winded and couldn't do any better than a short lope.

A hundred yards short of the ruins, Snip stepped into a sand rathole and started down. He staggered and wallowed, trying to keep his legs under him, but he was too tired. He lost his front legs, went down, and rolled. Gil kicked his feet out of the stirrups and pushed himself out of the saddle, just as Snip nosed over, did a flip, and landed on his back. Gil rolled clear and jumped to his feet.

The men were coming up the canyon. Gil ran to Snip and tried to get him up, but he lay there, gasping for breath and blinking his eyes. He was lying on his right side, on the Henry rifle.

He had to get the rifle! He grabbed the stock and struggled with it. He begged Snip to get up. The men were drawing closer and firing their guns. Bullets zinged through the air and kicked up sand all around him.

He left the Henry and ran for his life. He made a dash for the ruins, staying low to make himself less of a target. He could heard the horses behind him now, and the sharp crack of gunfire.

Something struck him in the leg, and his knee collapsed under him. He hit the ground, got up, and tried to run. He couldn't feel his leg, and it dangled like a broken stick. He fell into the sand and started crawling.

He could hear Trumbull's voice now, and he knew he would never make it to the stone walls. He turned, drew his pistol, and prepared to make his last stand.

They came toward him, thundering up the canyon. Gil had four shots left in his pistol. He would let them get closer before he fired. He would use three shots, and if he failed to stop them, he would save the last one for himself. He waited for them to come into range.

They were fifty yards away now and closing fast. Forty yards. Thirty. He could see the other man now, and recognized the skinny neck, the long chin, the toothless mouth, and the grape eyes. It was Junior. They were ducking behind the necks of their horses, giving him almost nothing to shoot at. He lined up Trumbull in his sights and waited for a shot.

Out of the corner of his eye, he saw a flash of color and a blur of motion. William dashed out from behind some rocks and leaped up on Trumbull's back. The horse shrieked in fear and began to rear. The two men tumbled off the horse and landed on the ground.

They rolled and William came up on top. He seized Trumbull's throat in his left hand, picked up a rock in his right, and slammed it down, once, twice, three times.

Junior didn't have time to aim his shotgun and fired from the hip. Fire leaped from the gun and the buckshot peppered the ground. The gun roared again, struck William, and sent him flying through the air.

Gil took careful aim with both hands, lined up the sights on Junior's chest, and squeezed the trigger. When the smoke cleared, Junior's saddle was empty. He lay on the ground. Gil cocked the pistol and waited for someone to move. There was not a sound except the snorting of the horses and the rustle of the wind. All three men lay motionless.

He could feel a dull pain in his leg. His pants were soaked with blood. He ripped off a piece of his shirt and made a tourniquet just above the knee. He crawled toward the men, ready to fire at the first sign of movement. Junior had been struck in the heart and was dead, his toothless mouth wide open.

Gil crawled over to Trumbull. A glance at the bloody mass where a face had once been told him that C. D. Trumbull would never cause trouble again. He crawled over to William and saw the pattern of buckshot on his chest. William lay on his back, his golden eyes glazed and staring at the sun. He was dead.

Gil knew he was losing strength. He would have to hurry. He caught Snip, tied a rope onto William's ankles, and dragged him to the base of the lookout mountain. Looking up to the top, he wondered if he could make it. There was a narrow, winding path up to the top. Maybe old Snip could climb it.

They started up, dragging William behind them. Snip picked his way up, staggering and lunging over the rocks. Gil urged him on, spurring him with his good leg. At last Snip lunged one last time and they stood on the flat top of the mountain.

A strong wind blew over the top, whistling through the rocks and whispering in the grass. Gil could see the entire Canadian River valley spread out before him, mile after mile of empty prairie, with puffs of white clouds racing over it. He slid out of the saddle, dragged William to the south edge of the mountain, and propped his back against a big rock. He saw Vicki's flute tucked into William's belt, and he placed it in the stiff fingers.

He stepped back and looked at him for a long time. He ran his eyes over the long black hair blowing in the wind, the proud head now gray in death. "You're home now, William. Play forever. Good-bye."

He was feeling weak and dizzy, but he mustered the strength to crawl into the saddle. Snip picked his way down the mountain. Gil fought against the dizziness and tried to think about what he should do. If he didn't find help, he would die. Trumbull and Junior must have had a base camp somewhere close by. Maybe there were other hunters in the valley. What would Ben Woolsey have done in this situation?

He found the horses standing over their dead masters. He threw their reins over their necks and drove them down the valley. He tied Snip's reins in a knot and held onto the saddle horn. No matter what happened, he had to hold on. Snip trotted along behind the other horses, and Gil slumped forward in the saddle.

Hours passed, and at last Snip stopped. Gil opened his eyes and saw five or six buildings of picket and sod construction. At first he thought he was dreaming, but then a man came out of one of the buildings and came over at a fast walk. He was a small, wiry man with long black hair, a sharp nose, and friendly eyes.

"You're wounded, man, what happened? That's Trumbull's horse there, and that one belongs to his thieving friend. What's going on?"

"They were killed," Gil whispered.

"Indians?"

He shook his head.

The man pulled him off the horse and helped him into one of the buildings. He laid him down on a buffalo robe and covered him with a smelly blanket.

"Where am I?"

"Hideville is what we call it. It's a buffalo camp, and the

only civilization between Dodge City and Fort Griffin. You're a lucky man that you found us. Who are you?"

"Gil Moreland." He looked into the man's face and tried to keep him in focus. "Please get me back to Weatherford." He removed the chain and gold coin from around his neck and handed them over. "Please help me. I must see Martha again."

"Just take it easy, Gil Moreland. I'll get some help for that leg." He stood up and started to leave, then he stopped. "What happened to Trumbull and Junior? Did you kill them?" Gil nodded. "God bless you, man! You've done the world a service. They murdered one of our best men three days ago."

Other men came and looked at his leg. They discussed it in low voices. They washed it and filled the wound with warm tallow and wrapped it in a clean dressing. They gave him broth and told him he needed to build up his strength. He drank the broth and fell asleep.

The next day they came again. He studied their faces as they pulled off the dressing. Johnny, the man who had come out to take him off the horse, stared at the wound and chewed his lip. The other man's expression was grave.

"You need a doctor," said Johnny, "but we don't have one. It would take five or six days to get you to Dodge, and you might not make it."

They packed the wound with herbs and tallow and wrapped it again. It throbbed in the night, and Gil could no longer feel his toes. The next day the hunters checked it again. They stepped outside and talked in whispers. When they returned, Johnny came up and put his hand on Gil's shoulder.

"Would you rather die with both legs or live with one?"

Gil felt fear crawling down his spine. "I want to live."

Johnny gave his shoulder a squeeze. "We'll do our best.

We ain't doctors, but Elias"—he tilted his head toward the other man—"helped take some off during the war."

Elias stepped up. "We've got some laudanum you can take."

"I don't want it."

"It'll kill the pain."

"I don't want it."

The two men glanced at each other, and Johnny said, "What about whiskey?"

"Bring me a barrel of it."

Johnny smiled.

They left, and while they were gone, Gil looked at his leg. It had turned blue-black around the wound, was swollen, suppurating, and ugly, and it gave off a horrible odor. But he would miss it.

The men came back. Johnny carried a crock jug and poured out a glass of corn whiskey. Gil drank it down and held out the glass for more. Johnny talked softly about an uncle of his down in Texas who had made whiskey. Johnny talked, Gil drank, and Elias scrubbed a butcher knife and a meat saw with soap and water.

Gil tried not to stare at the saw, but he couldn't help it. There was a certain fascination about looking at the device and thinking that, in a few minutes, it would be used to cut off his leg.

There was a long silence. Johnny had run out of things to say. They all listened to the sound of Elias' knife on the whetrock. Gil's head was swimming. He looked at his leg and began to cry. "I don't want to lose it."

Johnny took his hand. "I know you don't." He glanced over his shoulder. "Elias, let's go. He's ready." He looked into Gil's eyes. "I'm going to sit on your chest and pin down your arms. Close your eyes and grit your teeth and think of something else. It won't take long and you won't see any of it. Are you ready?"

Tears flowed down Gil's cheeks and into his ears. He nodded. Elias stood a few feet away, holding the saw and knife behind his back. Johnny climbed over Gil's chest and pinned his arms to the bed.

Gil stared into Johnny's face. His teeth were set on edge and beads of sweat stood out on his lip and forehead. He felt the knife circle his leg, going deeper and sending dull pain shooting up his thigh. Then he heard the saw and felt it grinding at his bone.

"Don't do it," he screamed. "No, please, no, I want my leg!"

Johnny tried to calm him, tried to hold his arms down, but Gil threw him over backward and sent him rolling across the floor. He raised up and reached for his leg.

Elias was holding it by the ankle. He gave his head a shake and carried the leg outside. Gil cried out and fell back, unconscious.

For two weeks he hovered between life and death, tossing on bedding that smelled of his sweat and oil. He had fever dreams that were vivid and terrible. He saw William in some of the dreams. He heard Vicki's flute. He dreamed of his boyhood on the frontier. He dreamed that Martha was standing over him, cooling his brow with a damp cloth.

Then one morning he awoke and saw things clearly: the picket walls chinked with mud, the cottonwood ridgepole, the branch-and-dirt ceiling, the hard-packed earth floor. He sat up. His leg was covered with a wool blanket.

He threw back the blanket and saw the stump, wrapped in a white bandage. Beside him, sitting on the floor, was a pot of stew, still warm. He lifted it to his lips and drank the broth.

He looked at his arms. They were thin and white. He saw

a mirror hanging on the wall across the room and he crawled to it. He used a chair for support and climbed up to a standing position. It was very strange, standing on one leg.

He looked at himself in the mirror and was shocked at the face he saw. It was not his. His saw his father and his grandfather and his great-grandfather looking back at him. The face was gaunt and bearded, and the eyes had the look of a forty-year-old man. He began to feel shaky and sat down in the chair.

Johnny walked in at that moment. "Gil, you're alive, we didn't kill you after all! You're a tough dobber. We gave you up several times."

Gil tried to smile. "What's the date?"

"Sometime around the middle of August, I would reckon."

"The middle of August," he murmured. He had left Weatherford in May. "When do you suppose I can leave?"

"Be patient, my man. Give yourself plenty of time. As a matter of fact, you're in luck. We've got so many flint hides stacked around Murry's store, someone will have to haul a load to Dodge, probably within two weeks. If you're strong enough, you can go." He dug into his pocket and came out with the gold coin and chain. "Here, this belongs to you. The day you rode in here, you told me to keep it for you."

"It's yours. My mother put it around my neck when I left home. She said I should use it to save my life. You saved my life, and it belongs to you."

"I didn't do it for gold."

"I know you didn't, but you earned it."

"Maybe so," Johnny nodded. He went out the door and came back with a crutch. "Me and Elias thought you might need this. We whittled it out of a piece of dead bodark and ruined three good knives, it was so hard. It'll never break, I'll wager."

Gil took the crutch and ran his hand over the dark bodark, which had been peeled and shaved smooth. The shoulder piece was covered with a scrap of cotton cloth. "That's nice, Johnny. Thank you. I'll start practicing with it right away."

By the time the hide wagon set out for Dodge City, Gil was getting around on his crutch. He climbed up on the wagon seat without help. The wagon pulled out of Hideville, and Gil waved good-bye to his friends.

As they climbed out of the valley of the Canadian River, he gazed off to the east and saw the lookout mountain in the distance, blue in the morning haze. He watched the mountain until it passed out of sight, and then he faced the front and his thoughts turned toward home.

20

It was around the first of October when he stepped out of the freight wagon that had taken him the last twenty miles from Fort Worth to Weatherford. The trip had taken more than a month.

He watched the six oxen plod on down the dusty street. He fitted the crutch under his arm and went stumping down the street toward Mrs. Valkenburg's house. People stared at him, but they didn't recognize him. He wore a beard now. His hair was longer, his face thinner, and there was something different in his eyes.

He was anxious to see Mrs. Valkenburg again. She would grieve over his missing leg, but she would get used to it. He wouldn't allow her to treat him as an invalid. Pearl would be another matter. She would try her best to spoil him.

He was getting around well on his crutch, and as soon as the stump of his leg healed over, he would get one of the local craftsmen to build him a peg leg of good Parker County oak.

He stopped in front of the house and stared. The smile faded from his lips. The windows were boarded up, and tall weeds and grass grew in the yard. He hobbled up the steps and through the yard gate, which hung on one hinge. He went through the yard and up the porch steps.

He banged on the door and waited. No one answered. The house was silent. All at once he understood that Mrs. Valkenburg had died, and he was afraid—afraid because things had changed and moved on without him.

He made his way down the steps and through the gate and stopped on the edge of the street. He thought about Mrs. Valkenburg. They had not always gotten along, but she had been a good mother to him. He wondered if she had died in her chair by the window, waiting for him. He grieved for her.

He went on down the street and turned on the lane that led to Martha's house.

The oak tree in the yard had turned a golden brown. He paused at the gate and stared at the glider swing, trying to remember Martha's face. He went up the flagstone walk and up the steps, across the porch and to the door. He knocked.

Mrs. Wynn did not recognize him. She must have thought he was a peddler or a beggar. She kept herself behind the door.

"Mrs. Wynn, I've come back," he said. "I want to see Martha."

"You've come . . ." Her eyes narrowed and she studied his face. "Oh, please, go away and leave her alone! Hasn't she suffered enough?"

"I understand how you feel, but I must see her."

"She doesn't live here anymore."

He stared at her. "She . . . doesn't live here anymore?"

"No, Gil Moreland, she has moved, she's gone."

"Did she marry?"

Mrs. Wynn glared at him. Her lips trembled. "Yes, she married. Of course she married. Did you expect her to wait around until you finished playing on the frontier? Your mother waited. She died waiting. Now you've finally come back and there's nothing left, is there?"

"No, there's nothing left," he said. "Thank you, Mrs. Wynn."

His crutch made a loud thump on the wooden porch. He picked his way down the steps and was out in the yard when he heard her voice.

"Wait."

He stopped and looked back at her. Her gaze seemed to go through him, and she held her hands clasped in front of her. She came down the steps and out into the yard.

"She's here for a visit. Maybe she'll want to talk to you, I don't know. I can ask if you wish."

"Thank you. I would appreciate it."

"Wait here." Her eyes went to his stump, and it appeared that she wanted to ask about it, but she turned and went back into the house.

The walk out to the Wynn house had tired him, so he went to the glider swing and sat down. He listened to the wind whispering in the dead leaves. Somehow it reminded him of William. He heard footsteps and looked up into Martha's clear blue eyes.

"Hello, Gil."

He pushed himself up on the crutch. "Hello, Martha."

She came over and sat down in the swing. He sat down beside her and laid his crutch on the ground. Neither said anything for a long time. Now and then he stole a glance at her out of the corner of his eye. She had changed. She looked older. She was still beautiful, but in a more subdued way. There seemed an air of sadness in her eyes.

"I'm teaching school now," she said. "I have a little school out in the Willow Springs community. Father thought it would . . . Did Mother tell you about James?"

"No."

She sighed and looked into her hands. "I didn't wait for you, Gil. I just couldn't. James and I were married in June.

He had promised me that he would give up horse racing. Maybe that was too much to expect. On the Fourth of July we went to a picnic. There were many horses, and in the afternoon the men started matching. James went home and got his mare.

"I thought it would be all right, just one more time. He had been good about it and I knew how much he loved to race. The mare fell near the finish line and James was crushed. He lingered for two days."

"I'm sorry, Martha. You've deserved the best in life, but you haven't gotten it. It isn't fair."

She studied him for a moment. "No, it isn't fair." Her eyes went to his bad leg. "What happened to you, Gil?"

He told her about his trip north, the death of William, and how he had lost his leg in the buffalo camp. She listened to the story and nodded.

"It seems we've both been treated badly." She had been holding a white handkerchief in her left hand. Now she unfolded it and brought out his mother's ring. "I kept it for you. Here."

He reached out to take it but drew back his hand. "I have no use for it. Would you keep it for a while?"

Their eyes met. "If I keep it, what does it mean?"

"It doesn't mean anything, unless you want it to mean something. Martha, let's try again. I've changed."

She nodded. "Yes, but so have I. Sometimes I feel dead inside. Maybe teaching school is enough. Maybe those are the only children I'm supposed to have. I don't know anymore." She turned the ring over in her hand. "I don't want to be hurt again."

He reached out his hand and placed it on her shoulder. "I don't want you to be hurt again either. Martha, I thought about you so much. You were the only reason I wanted to live. I came back for you."

She gave him a sad smile. "Gil, if we tried it again, it wouldn't be easy. I'm demanding. I don't want what everyone else has. I want something better."

"I'm willing to try it if you are."

She placed the ring back in the handkerchief and folded it up. "Well . . . can you stay for supper?"

"Is it safe, with your mother?"

She glanced into his face and saw that he was smiling. "I can't make any guarantees, but she's never hit a one-legged man before."

He laughed at that and pulled her into an embrace. "Fair enough. I can't ask for better odds than that."

They sat together in the swing, watching the sun slide down below the horizon. It bathed the prairie country in golden light. They stood up and walked toward the house. Martha walked at his pace and supported him with her arm, even though he didn't need it.

At the porch, Gil stopped and looked again at the golden sunset. He saw William's eyes in the sun and heard his flute music in the wind.

Martha helped him up the steps and they went inside.